Dedication

To my beloved Wife and Son, Melanie and Oscar.

Acknowledgment

Sincere thanks to my family and friends who have listened patiently, over the years, to my stories (and that one day I would write them down) and always with encouragement. I also want to thank my cancer care team; without you, I wouldn't be able to write Bonsai's story. I love you all.

I can't think of a better way to encapsulate my overall sentiment of thanks, and why I love stories, than to share with you the background of the cover art to this novel.

I was in Stanford Hospital a few years ago receiving a bone marrow transplant to extend my life from the onset of blood cancer. Rationally or irrationally, I am not sure which, I felt concerned that maybe I wouldn't be able to walk the hills of my much-loved home country of Scotland with my family again and especially my son, who was 13 at the time. So, my next best thing was to search the internet for Scottish landscape artists. I sought out a picture we could look at together; albeit in California, I found a painter that spookily came from my village in Scotland, Charles Randak. I contacted him and bought one of his pictures that I loved. When I returned from the hospital, it was there waiting for me. The scene in the picture has a lady on a beach looking out to sea, Westward. I liked to think she was missing someone, or trying to understand something from the sea in front of her, I liked to think she was searching with some hope, to reconnect with something, life maybe. At least that was my interpretation of his picture. Ultimately, the image drove my imagination to think of Bonsai, a story that revolves around the passage of time and life and things that are not always in the character's control.

We kept in contact, Charles and I. I wrote to him and told him I had written a novel, a year or so later after the delivery of that picture. I asked if he would paint the sleeve of the novel. I thought it was a long shot, for an unpublished author (we have never met after all) but I was thrilled he said yes. He read the novel and used his imagination to create the portrait of the character Lilly from my story which you can see on the sleeve.

I love the serendipity of that story and in the most challenging of circumstances. As I say, it both encapsulates the sentiment of Bonsai and how I see life and for that matter, how consequential storytelling is. Its importance, at least for me, is paramount.

I hope like Charles, Bonsai will provoke a picture in your own mind's eye that may somehow inspire you, even in the smallest of ways. If nothing else, I am sure it might encourage you to buy a lottery ticket!

Contents

Dedication iii

Acknowledgment iv

Prologue viii

Chapter 1 A Brief Introduction To Bonsai And Where He Was Once Upon A Time 1

Chapter 2 A Very Small Peak At Ly Years Later And More On Where Bonsai Was 21

Chapter 3 Let's Meet Lily In Person 58

Chapter 4 How Lily Met Lauren 90

Chapter 5 Lauren's secret 98

Chapter 6 How Bonsai Met His Friend 112

Chapter 7 Bonsai Tells Monty His Truth 123

Chapter 8 Lauren Is Not Happy About Her Golf Assignment 146

Chapter 9 Are You Ready For The Tournament, Bonsai? 163

Chapter 10 Takeshi Is On His Way, And Bonsai Remembers How He Met Ly 173

Chapter 11 How We Made Lily At Pfeiffer Falls 182

Chapter 12 After Pfeiffer Falls, Bonsai has to hustle 193

Chapter 13 How Did Bonsai Hide Moses? 213

Chapter 14 Welcome Lily, Goodbye Ly 218

Chapter 15 The Source Of Lauren's Pain 225

Chapter 16 Takeshi's Perspective When Ly Returns From Pebble Beach In 1979 234

Chapter 17 Takeshi's Bird Lands, And His Driver Awaits 245

Chapter 18 Lily takes Lauren to corporate entertainment at the Golf Tournament 255

Chapter 19 It Was Takeshi's Wish That You Accept This 265

Chapter 20 Lauren Discovers The Wild Goose Chase, And Lily Finds What She Lost 272

Chapter 21 Never mind the leaders; we are following a different story, folks. 282

Chapter 22 Meet me in the Rose Garden 287

Postscript 293

About The Author 295

Prologue

I was just talking to a friend the other day from Scotland. A guy I used to work with.

He shared with me he had just been on vacation.

He had traveled from San Francisco to Los Angeles with his kids.

His wife and his kids.

They had a great time.

It was one of the best holidays they have ever had, so he said anyways.

They needed that break apparently, for various reasons, that we don't need to get into much detail on.

You might care less about going to California, maybe some other place is more your family's thing and, so let me get to the point.

"You stopped for gas on your way from San Francisco to Los Angeles?" I asked my friend.

"Sure, that is a funny thing to ask".

"Of course. We stopped, let me think, at a town off the

Highway. The 101? The town name began with an "S", I think".

"Where John Steinbeck was from. You know that author".

"I know Salinas. I am a bookworm, after all. Erm, can I ask you one more thing?"

"Sure. Go ahead. Is it going to be another weird question?"

"When you stopped for gas?"

"Yeah, what?"

"Do you remember the guy that served you? You know his or her name? What did they look like, for instance?"

"Are you crazy? Of course not. No, I don't remember the server. Who remembers a gas station server and what they look like? A regular gas station worker. Do you really remember who served you in any retail place, for that matter?"

That conversation inspired this story. What if someone you didn't notice today had a truly remarkable story and you didn't realize? And that is true, of Bonsai.

Chapter 1

A Brief Introduction To Bonsai And Where He Was Once Upon A Time

There is something inherently childish about spitting. And it maybe has a masculine thing to it, too.

In old movies, at least, a character may spit to exhibit a show of machismo. It may just be me, but it just feels like it is something that is from a previous time.

Do people spit these days? Maybe they do, just not in my crowd.

Young adolescent men, hanging around, with no place in particular to go. In the United States, anywhere kind of town before cell phones, say the 1950s, talking to each other awkwardly in groups and punctuating their sentences with a spit on the floor, like exclamation points.

For whatever reason, that is what I think about when I think about spitting. There is almost a sentimental side to that "old school" type of spitting,

What I am saying is it is a habit that has long since died out, but for the habitual spitting of over-hydrated sports players, mostly in soccer games today. Or baseball coaches spitting out chewing tobacco.

The type of spitting that exists today is generally a perfectly passive act, getting a taste out of your mouth, a functional act, in other words. The old-school kind of spitting I am talking about was a gesture, that is to say, it was part of a vocabulary of sorts.

Now, spitting at someone, not least in the face, is altogether a different thing in so many ways whether it's old times or present, the same applies.

Using spitting as a weapon, well, that has an animalistic feel to it. It conjures up the image of, say, a cat or snake hissing, an aggressive, distressed, defensive action that is both aggressive and, for some animals, it's the delivery mechanism for the venom that takes out their prey or attacker as the case may be. In the human world, though, it's used very rarely in that context. Personally, I can only think of the mobster's girl in old movies, showing their disgust at the arrest of their man, spitting on the cop or private detective in disgust.

Whether spitting is no longer in vogue or not, I think we would all agree that in the real world, spitting at someone in the face is a pretty unsocial and obnoxious act, either now or in the past. In fact, if it's you who is sharing your DNA with someone in that way, you better be sure your recipient isn't going to belt you right back

Bonsai

or worse! It's a pretty rude attack for a human in any circumstance.

It just so happened that in the second decade of the 21st century, a petty criminal known as "Toad" thought a spit in the face of those who dare cross his path would be a suitable trademark to make his mark. A calling card, if you will.

Toad was no young man, but no throwback to the 1950s either. He wasn't exactly sure what his age was, but in 2010, he was probably about 30. If you asked him what his age was, he wouldn't have a clue. He would have to try and get a number of some kind through adding up various stints inside and even then, he had maxed out at third-grade math and may still get stumped. You might even anger him if you asked. I wouldn't advise it if you wanted to have a pleasant day. But one thing was for sure, he could still spit with the accuracy of a third grader in the school yard. Just one of those strange things that, if you were curious, may, well, strangely impress you.

Presently, his spitting victim was "Bonsai". A fifty-something, down on his luck, Korean American Gas Station owner in Salinas that had once upon a time been pretty good otherwise at cards. "Had been" being the appropriate description. He was still a darn good mechanic, but that'd only be useful if he had customers! He was one of those locals that everyone knew. He had been there like an old sofa, forever there, but no one really knew or rather, made an attempt to know him. He was just known as that strange gas station guy, inoffensive but a bit odd, which would be a typical description if they were asked.

Unless you studied his trade license certificate on his store entrance, no one knew his real name, where he came from, what he liked or didn't. No one cared to ask, not in a mean way, but they just didn't. Even the origin of his nickname had long since disappeared with the tides. He was just "Bonsai", the old Asian guy that ran the gas station on the edge of Salinas. And that was if someone paid any attention whatsoever, which, for the most part, as I say, they really didn't.

But a rather long time ago, Bonsai was a guy who someone like Toad would never have had the audacity to spit at. As I introduce Bonsai to you, in those days, or for that matter, if you happened to find yourself in this particular gas station back then, passing through town, you would find that particularly hard to believe. You will just have to trust me on that for the time being - this guy used to have a much higher standing. And maybe he was going to again!

"Toad" wasn't the real name, of course, of the saliva organ donor of sorts with 1950s sensibilities. Of course, it hadn't been given to him in a kind way by his mother or a friend, let's say. Who calls someone "Toad" kindly?

Bonsai

No one was really sure who gave him that name but most agreed that it was perfect for him. Somehow, somewhere, someone said it and it stuck; "Toad". To be honest, I don't mean to be unkind, he looked reptilian, and he had a habit of puffing out his cheeks when talking (or spitting), you know, like a toad. There are many reasons it had been someone's bright idea, but like the throwback prehistoric namesake animal, the source of the nomenclature had been lost in time and it had just sort of stuck, and in a funny way, it now belonged to him.

Toad had led a remarkably predictable life for a Salinas born thug.

In another world, if someone, say a teacher or office manager, had pushed him - what would be the one noteworthy story for him to share? You know his "icebreaker" at a school discussion or business function, the dinner party time filler before desert, the airplane companion story, it would undoubtedly be the time he and his buddy "the Noose" tried to leap from the Pond, so to speak. That would be his life defining story.

You see, when Toad was 14, he came up with the idea to rob the local bank, the high street bank no less.

His accomplice, "Noose," was another antisocial kid who, at the time, was obsessed with Black Sabbath, and knives, and the paranormal and long tailed weasels in that order. Unlike Toad, though, he did have a level of cunning, the kind of cunning that, in principle, might make you good at the act of robbery or at least have the ability to plan one.

On the afternoon of the planned heist, they got stoned in Fort Ord National Park as usual.

It was some particularly strong weed that day, Toad had obtained it from his night shift working step father, who, as usual, was passed out on their sofa at 8 am that morning, making that particular piece of theft a walk in the park. They had ridden their bicycles there along the cycle path from home, skipping school as usual. From a distance, they may have looked like two perfectly fun-loving adolescents wearing hoodies and racing each other back and forth as they headed toward their spot on the edge of the dramatic Pacific Ocean. A scene from a movie, if you like, at least it looked like that from afar.

If a local kid saw them, though, they sure knew who they were and would get out of the way quickly. You didn't have to tell them twice that they were not good people. "Born evil," some might say. Or if a passing walker looked closely at the sinister wording on their sweaters or, for that matter, their cartoonishly evil faces too old for their bodies, they would be quick to conclude they were teenagers that were up to no good.

The Main Street Bank in Salinas was their target that day,

Bonsai

they decided, as they sat by their usual fire pit spot.

As he took his instructions, Toad threw rocks at seagulls that could smell their chips, hitting them with uncanny accuracy.

Noose's dad, a full-time alcoholic, had a handgun that Noose worked out would help the execution of their plan just fine. Noose explained to Toad it would be back in his dad's bedside drawer where he kept it before he even realized it was missing. Toad, half listening or following the plan, had turned his short attention span from hitting the impertinent visitors to starting a campfire with a zippo lighter and some dry beach wood.

The fire was quickly alight and the flames were full of praise for the brilliant act of bringing them to life. The red and orange flicker in the early evening light devilishly lit up Noose's face as he sketched out the details of the plan using a stick in the sand to illustrate the geography of the main street and their proposed entrance. A sketch in the sand was way more dramatic than sharing the plan on his Google Maps on his smartphone. When the last of his joint was finished, Toad took a moment to look at the early fall setting sun and his head was quickly full of dreams of a life beyond Salinas, which he could afford with that evening's impending winnings. I can't dwell on it, partly because Toad frankly doesn't really deserve it, but that was probably the most perfect moment of Toad's life!

Sandy Nicolson

The night that Noose had chosen for this adventure had been Halloween, of course. Noose opened his backpack and presented his partner with his mask for the heist.

It was a Teenage Mutant Ninja mask! If you are coming to this story, generationally apart from me, well, that was sort of a cartoon character from the 1990s.

Noose looked at his Casio and told his co-conspirator it was time to leave. Toad's adrenaline made his fingers tingle with excitement and for a moment it overrode the THC otherwise cursing through his veins. He was about to argue about why he was to be Raphael when Noose pulled the remaining item from his backpack. It was his father's glock. The sight of the gun caused Toad to pause. It was the first time Toad had seen a gun and he took it from his friend and his eyes widened immediately. His pupils dilated with love of the power they had in their presence. The gun was raised high towards his friend like a cross to the sky, and he smiled menacingly.

His friend simply smiled back and said teasingly, "so why don't you kill me?" Toad resisted the invitation, and stuffed the pistol inside the top of his jeans, and tightened his Harley Davidson buckle belt.

"Make sure you have the safety on, and mind the potholes," his friend joked as they headed back towards the town that night with speed and the light failing. "Don't blow your balls off, Toad!" It was the most sentimental exchange they had ever had.

Toad thought of himself as a blood thirsty slave catcher on a horse from years long gone as they peddled with gleeful speed toward their prize.

Noose's plan had worked perfectly at achieving anonymity, he thought smugly, as they slipped through the familiar town and soon found themselves in the high street dressed in their elementary Halloween Teenage Mutant Ninja Turtle masks.

Noose was good on details and had checked and the bank was to close at 6. He glanced at his watch as they jumped from the bikes, which they didn't bother to lock up as they parked them next to a bench in the pedestrian precinct. The trick or treating had kicked in, in earnest. The precinct was packed with children and families in costumes as they enjoyed the usual custom in the town of going between stores to collect candy.

Toad was to be the stickup man. It was agreed that Noose was to do all the talking. If they asked for five thousand dollars in unmarked bills, it was less likely the Police or anyone else for that matter would really give a crap a few weeks later, Noose had concluded this important fact from reading the local newspaper police reports. The local police were under-resourced and had far bigger gang crimes to solve at that time. But for Noose and Toad, five thousand dollars may be enough to start the beginnings of their very own cartel, or the ownership of the High School dope market at least. The "unmarked" bills request he had heard in some movie as a must in these situations!

Surprisingly, the actual childish robbery went more smoothly than you could imagine at first. Noose had later looked back forlornly that they hadn't actually needed his father's pistol, but it had made a huge difference to their sentence, according to the Judge.

As they entered the bank, the clock above the teller station told them if they weren't so buzzed that it was five minutes before closing. Just as Noose had supposed, there were no customers whatsoever. As they entered the last remaining teller working, they looked up from their smartphone and had supposed that this was simply two kids looking for candy. No need to sound an alarm, he had thought.

"Sorry, kids; we don't really have much candy to offer except this small bowl," he said, pointing to a meager and much-depleted bowl to the left of his station.

But when Noose spoke, the teller recognized with an instinctive cringe, "It's Noose's voice". He preferred to remember him as Michael Murphy, not the guy known for his ability to make hangman nooses in the third grade. He was a bad kid from kindergarten who was nearly (and should have been expelled) for setting the toilet block on fire as he graduated fifth grade. Michael had been three years below him in high school, and this kid was in the same year as his younger brother. His own mother had warned them that nothing good would ever come from that Michael boy. Sure enough, his mother was right. So, he instantly knew that nothing good was going to come from his entering the bank at this hour on Halloween, whichever way he looked at it, there was trouble afoot. His instinct was completely confirmed, of course, when he saw that his sidekick had drawn a gun and it didn't look like a toy either. Noose was saying something like, "It's not that type of candy we are here for!"

When he had to fill in the report, he would tell police afterward that he was certain they would be caught quickly anyway, particularly as he knew it was Michael (he didn't undermine the virtuosity of this by adding the other half which was that he was only paid minimum wage) and there was no way he was therefore going to refuse their request, much less tackle them. The notetaking cop told him this was indeed an open and shut case and added, somewhat pompously, that he was a brave young man. In the end, his nerves about having to justify quickly handling over the requested $5,000 dollars were unneeded. There was even a mention that he might be in for some reward money himself (which never came). Anyways, he had, after all, sounded the alarm immediately after they had left the bank and that was a good thing apparently.

Afterward, the robbers had taken off at speed on their steel horses to Toad's house. Everything had gone to plan, according to Noose until they reached Toad's house. Toad's mother was out "working" , Halloween was one of her busiest nights in the downtown dance bar she worked in. All the absent fathers would take refuge there, of course, ironically to see "wives" without costumes.

In all the excitement of the day and no doubt impacted by his stoned state, Toad had forgotten his house keys. Noose insisted they needed to take refuge there inside, he couldn't risk going back home. His father might well be there, and what if he had discovered the gun was missing before he had a chance to replace it? The adrenaline and THC were wearing off, and he was getting paranoid quickly.

Toad assured his friend it was fine, he could easily force open the back door with his brute strength, he had done it before. Sure enough, in short order, they were round the back of the trailer and he barged the back door. The latch gave away easily and soon they were inside. What could have been simpler? Phew.

Well, a neighbor named "Mary" complicated it unexpectedly. Mary was an Octogenarian with a faith that gave her a deep disdain for pagan Halloween traditions and so she was sitting on her back patio of sorts hoping the local kids couldn't tell she was in the house. After intermittently napping all day, she was now awake. Most importantly, for Noose and Toad, Mary was bored and a devotee of daytime police reality shows, a wannabe sleuth, a Murder She Wrote fan, you get the picture. She didn't see Toad and his 14-year-old friend, William, aka "Noose," who she had smiled at a thousand times, no that night she saw Rapheal and Michelangelo. Michelangelo was holding a pistol to boot when she saw him shoulder barge the kitchen door of her neighbor's house (who she ironically didn't care for) wide open, she knew she had a case to call in. She turned off her porch light and watched on as two turtle-headed folks, with a gun, unloaded a pile of cash onto the neighbors kitchen table.

She called 911 and told all this in excited, hushed tones to the Police.

As she told the Police, she wouldn't have otherwise called them, like I said, she couldn't care less for that lady (who brought strange men back at all hours of the night, you know) and howled like a wolf until dawn. No, it was the young boy she was worried about, without knowing, he was actually one of the intruders at the time, a Ninja Turtle, of all things.

A police car was dispatched, they didn't really have to do much at all, to their delight (it had been a long day), but instead entered through a still open kitchen door and found one boy smoking at the kitchen table with a wide grin and puffed out cheeks (he didn't write it up but the kid looked like a toad) and the other one bent over neat piles of hundred dollar bills. One of the easiest arrests he had ever made in the town.

"Don't even think about touching the gun!" he had instructed them, his own drawn, as he referred to the glock, lying now inert on the kitchen table.

Toad wasn't smart, but he wasn't that dumb to not comply.

And so, that is how Toad was introduced to the criminal justice system. Believe it or not, up until that point, he was incognito as a criminal mastermind in the making.

They were both given relatively "light" Juvenile Hall sentences on account of their age, but regardless, Toad's criminal education entered its freshman year that particular Halloween. There was a better ending for Noose, who was put into foster care, on release from Juvenile Hall and by all accounts, as we join you at the start of this story, is now an accountant in Sacramento, married with two children. So, he did get his wish to handle money that wasn't his. On the other hand, the only thing that had improved for Toad since then was his spitting technique.

Presently, Toad's spittal ball arced in the air like an archer's dart and "Bonsai," he mouthed as it hit the gas station owner with the same name.

The spitball landed like a warm snowball on his target's left cheek. It had been a while, naturally, since the fifty-something Gas Station owner had been spat on. I mean, how often does it happen to any 50-year-old Californian male? Like I said earlier, it's simply not a common thing to happen.

This was Toad's trademark, a childish attempt at a theatrical entrance. In some ways, it added color to an otherwise ostensibly routine day of driving door to door, in early 2010, either collecting debts or more generally bringing some muscle for their bosses, post-financial crisis in the Salinas Valley.

The spitting victim made no effort to touch his cheek from behind the counter. Thus, the spital presently slid down Bonsai's face and the slime soon hung from his chin, making him look like a drooling dog of sorts. He submissively accepted his master's henchman's uncourteous introduction.

Bonsai knew from experience that the alternative to wipe away the spittle in disgust, at least immediately, may lead to more theater from the thug they called Toad and he was hoping to avoid more serious drama on this particular day anyway. In the old days, in the days of the old Boss. This would never have happened. Of course, he wouldn't have been in this position. He wouldn't have lost. The cards wouldn't have dared to let him down. He had luck on his side then. He wouldn't have had a debt to be collected.

He was stoic about that aspect of the "old days", which, more specifically, was approximately ten years or so, in nearest proximity. It was just a different time. A time that had been kinder to him. Kinder to him, relatively, that is. In truth, outside of gambling and the sometime support of the small-time hoodlum Captain, it had been thirty years since the apex of Bonsai's life, but we will get to that.

He didn't know this for sure, but he consoled himself that it was like working for the same corporate organization for a long time in some office block in the middle of nowhere. In other words, there are the initial years, full of hope and promise, the functional years where you sort of get on with it, and unless you do something crazy good or bad, leadership forgets about you and then there are the closing years, where the snow melts and the new budding grasses break through and push past the decay that middle management has become and make it harder for the old to hang on, they have to be let go.

The change agency of life. He simply accepted that he had reached the closing years, and either way, his lot was what it was. There had at least been good times, at one point, however short lived. Maybe some people never get those. But ultimately, his time was pretty much up. He had pretty much reconciled to that at that point.

Bonsai

Toad was more of an unwelcome weed than fresh grass in the analogy that was running through his head, but otherwise, it held true. It was all about change. A stench of cigarette smoke and jalapenos from a recent roadside taco hung in the air as Toad's saliva wept from his chin.

Lost tourists looking for the local Steinbeck museum were the only other likely visitors to disturb this scene now in this otherwise dead-end, godforsaken gas station.

Driven from their hotels in Monterey in air-conditioned buses, maybe stopping for lunch at a local winery, those types of tourists would fly home to faraway places in Europe or Asia and tell their friends about the beauty of Salinas that had, afterall, been captured perfectly by Steinbeck and any short visit to his gas station to fill up the hire car would, of course, be forever forgotten.

The more profitable rush hour of long-haul truckers moving artichokes out East had happened a lifetime of hours before this scene. Around 5 am, to be precise. Serving the truckers had been the lifeline of keeping the garage afloat financially since Bonsai started work there under his Uncle all those years before. But there was no chance of seeing those folks at this hour.

They were Bonsai's favorite clientele and not just because they paid. As true as the Sun rose in the East, at 5 am, the truckers would be full of cargo and ready for Bonsai to fill their chariot's tanks with gas. It was a world he had always belonged in. The gas man. The gas wizard. The man with the pump. He marshaled the trucks through the pump lanes with great accuracy. In and out of his station, they went every day, directed by him as if he were an air marshal. He ensured no delays. No tank left without a completely full tank. They were filled precisely with the right grade of gas, at one point at the best price in the valley. And, of course, their paperwork was immaculate and ready for collection as they departed like travelers from a time past with immaculate visa papers destined for distant lands; New York City, Las Vegas, and Miami with cargos of the freshest produce. Artichokes to be made into gazpacho soups, abalone and fresh crab from Monterey Bay and pinot's from the Salinas Valley to be served on the finest white tablecloths in restaurants where powerful people made decisions that changed the world. In a small way, don't thank the waiter, the restaurateur, your host even, thank Bonsai in Salinas, whose gas made this meal possible.

In his 20-plus years at the station, he had gotten to know most of the old-time drivers and become fast friends with many of them. As the years went by and they became part of National Organizations despite their respective corporate requirements to use chain gas stations, for a time, many of them flouted the requirements and came to Bonsai's station, some of them to the point of almost losing their jobs.

Bonsai

There was something about the transient nature of the trucks, perhaps, that made him so fond of them when they appeared out of the fields. Maybe, it was precisely because the drivers only knew him as the Gasman, which made him feel proud. Perhaps it was the discipline of filling the tanks, the responsibility, the fact he wouldn't spill a drop. Lives could be lost otherwise! The fact was he was completely focused on his tasks when the convoy came through, that was the highlight of his day. No time then to wallow in the past when the truckers came to fuel. Unlike, the rest of the day looking out of the window when the store was dead, full of melancholy about what could have been. No, the blues came later in the day.

He could not afford any such indulgence when the long haulers came through. Taking their precious cargos eastward. Keeping the country fed and watered. Keeping the country alive. No, Bonsai played an important part in all of that. He fed the metal horses. It gave him a purpose.

It was only later in the day when he would find himself lost and much later still at a card table at the back of some restaurant in town when everything else had otherwise closed. That was a snapshot of the highs to lows of Bonsai's daily life then. Then came this hangover that was an increasingly inevitable visit of the debt collectors the next day, if, as was usually the case, he lost.

And so, Toad today would come for their masters' payment.

Sandy Nicolson

And with that, the cycle of this day's reverie was broken. All he could do presently was let the spital, the grotesque reflection of the fact that he was in a losing cycle, run down his face and fall onto his gas station floor in leaking tap drips.

Chapter 2

A Very Small Peak At Ly Years Later And More On Where Bonsai Was

The memory of her past would come to her disjointed and out of sync, always.

Years later, in California, people would ask at dinner parties where she came from, where she really came from, and then the inevitable follow up question: what was it like in Asia in the 1960's? Her authentic answer that she never gave was that she didn't really remember.

She would give the crowd a story, something that would satiate them, make them talk for the first time as a couple in a while on the ride home about something that interested them, force them to make an exception to the usual spiel about the middle school baseball game, the neighbors shaky marriage, their eldest's upcoming piano recital, the Senator in the news that dared to run for Office despite his affair, no they would talk about her instead. What did you make of Takeshi's wife? She is interesting, don't you think? There is something about her I can't put my finger on.

Whatever story Ly Takeshi chose to give you, one thing was true, it was always make-believe, without exception.

Sandy Nicolson

It didn't matter what she chose to share, the only authentic memory of consequence that she wouldn't share, the only one that she knew was true, was the story of Bonsai and Takeshi. Even if she chose to share it, it would have been too complicated a story, too unbelievable, even for those conditioned by Hollywood in the West, to understand, much less believe. But it was, after all, the reason she was in their presence and had a daughter and of course, that was one piece of her life that was more important than anything else.

Bonsai looked at the digital clock on the cash register and it stubbornly clicked to 2:10pm. He took in the time in his mind's eye. He doubted he could have reached as low a point in his life as this. No one can control the cards they are dealt. He, of all people, knew that.

On paper, his story probably would have made some kind of logical sense. He as the son of an opium addict in Korea, escaped to the US as a young man thanks to the benevolence of an Uncle, he had fallen in love with someone that would never be his, had a child, raised the child on his own, forsaken any dreams of any other form of fulfillment to raise the child, developed a gambling habit somewhere along the way, won and lost and now presently found himself stuck in front of two small time debt collectors in Salinas in his decaying gas station.

So, if you really looked at the current predicament through

Bonsai

Bonsai's eyes, it was not really that surprising. He was sadistically letting this moment play out at this moment in his life's arc.

If it were his life movie, and this is where we join Bonsai, as much as he was tempting it, this is far from the "The End" title card for Bonsai. If you wait and see, maybe somewhere there is a path to redemption, a reason for hope. Stick with me, really. It's the point of the story. But you have to reach the bottom before you turn back in search of whatever the apex might be, that's what Bonsai was thinking deep down in his soul then. He just wasn't aware of that. He wasn't done yet, not yet no sir. At this present moment though, from the instant the characteristic Salinas Valley late afternoon sky that burned into this stage, it didn't look good for him. I don't know, but maybe that is what brought him off the canvas.

As if to ring a thought true, a fly buzzed loudly in the store to break the dark mood that these visitors had brought in. At least phonetically, the fly provided a reminder that the world was at least still moving on its axis, buzzing and alive, just about.

A truck teasingly hurled past on the highway to the left of the station, throwing up a cloud of dust as if insulting Bonsai further, on its way to a different station, some National Chain, no doubt. For a moment, Bonsai was reminded of a cowboy movie scene he couldn't put his finger on. He wanted to squint his eyes in the light like Clint Eastwood but restrained himself from the indulgence. He didn't have six shooters on his hip to blow these punks away without care anyway.

"How is your daughter these days?" Toad's boss snorted menacingly and ignored the delivery of his welcome spit; "hello."

Bonsai stayed still, like a mannequin. Inwardly, he took comfort that she was so far away from where they stood they would never see her star if they even had the telescope and celestial map.

"We know she is in San Francisco somewhere," drooled M, Toad's sidekick and technically his boss.

Bonsai let a pause take hold. He took in an audible breath and let out a sigh that had a meditative quality for him and irritated his guest in equal measure.

"You need to work on your lines," Bonsai quipped eventually.

He saw them thinking, and before they could work out a response, he added.

"I have a line of credit that just came in, an old boss of mine needs me to do some extra work. It will pay enough to settle my debt with interest".

M seemed relieved to have a question he could answer; "You know that your old line of credit died a long time ago;" and added by explanation; "his son is not as generous, as you know. Especially for a chink who can't play cards!" and then added; "Why don't you just mortgage this shit hole?" which he quickly realized was a rhetorical question.

Bonsai reassured himself with the thought of the many kids that would appear in the store shortly like clockwork as the school bell rings and consequently, this interview, for what it was, would likely run its course. The kids would disperse these goons, he thought. They would disrupt the scene with their presence.

M continued with the speaking role;

"You're too frequently late with your payments," and added, "We, like you, are not particularly fond of our day jobs and visiting this place isn't exactly the highlight of an otherwise shit existence".

Bonsai answered coolly, "Like I said, I will pay this debt. I just need a week to do a job".

M's voice was a completely different octave to Toad's, to the point where you had to really lean in to hear what he was saying. Bonsai wasn't sure if it was affected that way deliberately or not, but it was certainly irritating nevertheless.

Bonsai stared back at his dementors with a look that said, "What are you going to do about it?"

Sandy Nicolson

He looked at the Toad's boss's neck to amuse himself. It had a large "M" tattoo for "Mouse" scrawled across his neck and under his shirt to some level of a subterranean place below. Bonsai conjectured he got to know the thirteenth letter of the alphabet in the can. It hung across his neck like some kind of lazy spider. He never actually knew why he was nicknamed "Mouse". He had always known him as such. Was it his small frame, his soft annunciation, his ability to collect things for other prisoners like proverbial pieces of cheese in the can? Who knows? Like he was wandering around inconsequential television channels, he let the thought drift away just as Judge Judy was about to announce a verdict on the television behind his register. It seemed just as meaningless either way.

Whatever the reason, sure enough, M was branded like a piece of cattle.

Enough time had now passed for Bonsai to take a serviette from the store's coffee stand to the side of the cashier, next to a jar of fluorescent pink lollipops and wipe himself clean. The kind of jar of lollipops people would guess the number of at the church auction. He fleetingly thought of offering a lollipop to each of them in consolation for his lack of payment. Maybe a lollipop would appease these sulking children. He thought better of it.

The grouping of the old coffee machine and the candy jar on his counter suddenly looked to him like a miniature model of a

Bonsai

1970s power station complex he had seen once on television. The kind that, regardless of the news story, looked on the verge of catastrophe somewhere in Eastern Europe, that no one, at least watching, had ever been to, much less could point to on a map! He wiped the Toad slime off his face with the perfunctory accuracy of a barber toweling a customer after a shave.

"As I say, it bores me to visit you, Bonsai, you know that, and that is saying a lot," said M softy and with just the right amount of menace, like it was the type of line he practiced for these types of visits in a mirror at home.

The digital clock on the register clicked to 2.15, with the same intent as the blades of the fly buzzing around the store like a spectator.

M gave Toad a look that said, "Make my point".

Toad's eyes bulged in excitement at being given an order and a purpose. In a beat, Toad grabbed Bonsai by the neck and hurled Bonsai across the counter, taking out a display of Doritos that had been kindly set up in a triangular advertising display stand, shaped rather like a Christmas tree by that company's sales representative, a week or so ago. She had been a twenty-something college graduate who clearly had much higher expectations for her first year out of college than hanging packets of Doritos on a company pyramid display in a dead-end gas station in Salinas. This much was obvious to Bonsai from her surly disposition, like a server refilling coffee in a throwback diner when she already knew her tip was going to be meaningless.

Momentarily, Bonsai's head hit the ground with a thud.

Packets of Doritos were shaken across the floor like candy from a pinata. In short order, Bonsai's neck now hung in Toad's vice-like grip, three feet in front of his own counter, like a butcher showing a customer the last chicken for sale on his counter. As if for theatrical effect, Toad stood on a loose packet of "flaming hot chips", producing a louder than expected and threatening crunch of Dorito bones.

"That could be your neck breaking, understand me? We are not as forgiving as Citigroup," M added, as if much of a voiceover was needed to explain their intent.

Bonsai struggled to regulate his breathing through his nose, he had lost all capacity through his throat. As he hung there, he looked down at Toad's shoes, a pair of red Air Jordans. Strangely, the sight of them sharpened his consciousness, "as if this fat bastard ever played ball," he thought in his mind's eye.

"You know how important it is for you to pay your taxes on time? It's not polite to play cards with someone else's money. You better get the message. We will be filling our truck today on the

Bonsai

house, and if you don't pay by Monday, the boss says he's bringing the fleet to be watered, and we aren't going to stop drinking until your well is dry. You got it?" snarled M.

Bonsai suddenly recalled the Texas Hold'em game at Danny's laundry the previous week. He shouldn't have gone all in on that last hand, he knew better than to drink tequila, but regardless of the alcohol, he played these days like he wanted to lose. You could say that he had a death wish, or rather lost his interest in winning or losing, in short, in living.

Bonsai figured he had had enough of sadomasochism for the day and stretched out his right hand and, just reached the cash register with his second stretch. With an out of place friendly chime, the register was presently opened, and the mouth of the till presented the meager green notes representing the day's cash takings of the day. Even if they hadn't been meager, nobody paid with cash these days anyway. There was maybe two hundred dollars or so, far less than he owed, but it would appease the goons for now and restore the place to some civility before the children arrived.

Toad let go of his neck and. Bonsai momentarily flapped like a freshly caught sardine on the floor of his boat. Toad blew air into his cheeks and helped himself greedily to the contents of the register and, without prompt, announced.

"Yes, I will take a bag," and then proceeded to drop sticky

grabs of cash from the till and fill a plastic bag almost three-quarters full with mostly ones, fives, and tens.

"And thanks for reminding me;" he went on and filled a second bag with cartons of cigarettes.

"Bad for your health, they say," chimed in M with a private joke smile.

M's mousy eyebrows suddenly arched and his forehead muscles pinched forward. He did his best to impersonate an angry crustation illustration in a children's storybook. The archetypal small head, pink with no real room for anything that could master serious comprehension.

M looked with angst suddenly at the gas station forecourt. Bonsai followed his gaze as he stood up and gathered himself. Evidently, a cop car had pulled into the station forecourt. Momentarily, a solitary cop proceeded to get out and walk slowly to a pump as if in slow motion. Languidly, the cop started filling his wagon with gas. His pose made it look like filling the tank was some kind of break. He looked relaxed. He looked away from the store toward the artichoke fields that surrounded the store like he was a farmer contemplating the next time of harvest.

The patrol car was marked highway patrol, and Bonsai figured it was odd he didn't recognize him. He was most likely from

Bonsai

out of town. Monterey or Carmel, maybe. Naturally, he knew most of the cops in the valley. Most of them were regulars and he knew them by name but he intentionally didn't try to get any more familiar with any of them and in return, if they didn't know him other than superficially, if at all, it was just by name; "Bonsai!".

The fly buzzed as if an audience member were in the stalls, anticipating the next step of the actors on stage. Bonsai looked in unison with the other two as they looked out to the forecourt.

Bonsai's face, in contrast to concern, was rueful. If only a cry for help was, appropriate, to ring the proverbial bell and have these two losers immediately have the justice that was coming to them soon. If only he could commence some triggering violence, a clear sign that the store was under attack, raising the alarm or pulling his baseball bat from under his counter and start swinging!

Alas, Bonsai knew that raising the alarm now would only make matters worse. It wasn't these clowns he was afraid of or their boss, for that matter. It was that any trouble would get in the way of his plans. He did what he usually did when he was frustrated and pushed his hand through his hair. His hair was as thick and black as his teenage years, it bizarrely hadn't aged, like his hair had its very own ecosystem separate from the rest of his body. No, Bonsai knew to wait for now anyway. He had to be patient. If he wanted to climb out of the hole that was his current life that he so despised, he had to hold on.

"No funny stuff," M warned Bonsai, not knowing it was a superfluous thing to say, as he tracked Bonsai's gaze to the forecourt visitor, looking for clues of what his victim was thinking.

He added with extra effect, "If you love your daughter, my dwarf tree lover, you know what is best here for you".

"Toad, let's leave today's winnings here at our dear friend's Bank and we can return tomorrow".

"If you say so, señor M".

"Quick now," M added with the undertone of someone who had indeed been to the can and developed a godly fear of authority as a result.

Toad sneered at Bonsai as if he had planned it. He took two packets of cigarettes and left or rather dumped the rest of the bags behind the counter at Bonsai's feet.

Toad spat on the floor for theatrical effect to mark his imminent departure, Sort of his punctuation mark to signal the ending of this particular shake down. Bonsai took a quantum of relief that he hadn't looked for symmetry with his opening mark. A little variety with his spitting. As if they had practiced their steps, both of the goons turned and headed for the door, somewhat in sync, which made them look altogether ridiculous.

Bonsai

Bonsai looked on as the Police Officer finished his surveillance of the artichoke field and headed for the store. Somewhat surreally, the doorbell chimed like a wind chime welcoming him in. Bonsai wanted, of course, to ring the proverbial bell for help.

Looking at those two as they shuffled out of the store, the ghouls looked like an even more ridiculous pair.

M was not a tall man, 5 foot something, but skinny as a rake. He could have been a 12 year old kid. It was over 100 degrees outside, but he nevertheless wore a raincoat with a strap holding it together at the waist. Something he had likely found in a goodwill store and maybe thought it gave him the look of some gangster from a classic time. In contrast, Toad was oversized, well over 6 feet and 300 pounds. He looked like a bag of flour from behind.

If the cop had been worth something, he would have arrested them just because of their offensive appearances, but they ghosted past him as if they didn't exist in his world. Maybe if he had been local, he would have recognized these career criminals, but alas, it appeared they didn't even feature in his world.

The cop stood in front of Bonsai's desk and, in doing so, replaced; "dumb and dumber". He was a big man and clearly a man that worked out. What a waste, Bonsai thought, that he sat all day on his brains in that car.

Bonsai realized he had a bona fide customer of sorts in front of him again and promptly returned to character and functionally took the cop's fuel card from his outstretched hand and ran it through his machine mechanically.

It took a bit for Bonsai to shake the goons from his psyche, and it took a moment for him to realize the cop was asking him something; "How fresh is the coffee?" he was saying with a slightly accusatory tone.

The cop was pointing to the miniature power plant that was part of the coffee pot station, a stack of polystyrene cups and a range of radioactive coffee mate sachets. Next to it was a glass case proudly containing a range of donuts. As if Bonsai had forgotten where his coffee station was. Bonsai refrained from saying, "Well, this is not exactly Starbucks". Not because he was a cop, but more, because he felt a little drained, he restrained himself.

Instead, he replied courteously,

"Pretty fresh, and there is half and half in the fridge if you need it."

Bonsai added the half and half note, as if it were a luxury item reserved for special guests. He gesticulated towards the fridge at the rear of the store.

"Alright, coffee it is," and the cop proceeded to help himself.

Bonsai

He didn't ask about the freshness of the donuts in the glass case ironically. Instead, he helped himself to one with pink icing regardless (not bothering to use the tongs that lay by the case side, and frankly no one actually ever used).

There was a sense of unjustified entitlement though in this customer's case. The heat of the room melted the icing in a second of its release from the cake box to the unpurified air of the store. As the Officer immediately pulled at the donut's gelatine body with his greedy fingers, a children's picture book story style "gloop" of pink icing remained stuck to a frosted donut that had been its neighbor (for more than a few days). Something about the sight of the pink icing clinging to the other donut made Bonsai gag. He could still smell Toad's spit on his cheek, which made the reflex worse. The fly, who was feeling quite at home now, continued to buzz as the cop took a lifetime to locate the half and half. Flies are attracted to shit, Bonsai thought absently.

"Here, let me help you;" Bonsai came from around the front desk to show his visitor the Salinas Gas Station "white glove" service. As he did so, he kicked the bag of cash at his feet and instantly created a flood of green behind the counter. Bonsai suddenly felt a completely irrational fear. It was his money, after all, but nevertheless, he felt fearful of the scene he had created. It looked odd, seeing the cash laid out by his feet like a green river in Chicago on St Patrick's Day. In his mind's eye, it looked like he was in the process of robbing his own store.

"It's alright, I got it, I think I can find the milk," the cop said as if the offer of help was a slight on his detective skills.

Momentarily, the cop was right there by the till, proudly raising his polystyrene coffee cup in a toast with the see-through transparent bag with the sticky pink donut stuck inside it, which he held in his other hand. It looked like the cake was some kind of obtuse body part a pathologist had found on a murder scene or maybe a dead fish he had proudly caught earlier. Either way, it it was no elegant scene, Bonsai mused.

"Oh wonderful," he said warily; "Don't worry, officer, no charge for that, none whatsoever. We are grateful for your service."

Bonsai wasn't sure who else in the "we" he was referring to nor what service specifically he was commending or even had the right too, for that matter, even if he understood it was more a canned salute to service.

The Officer smiled thinly and then, like he felt obliged to return some sort of favor, he confided in Bonsai.

"Well, thank you," and adding, "You be careful;" and further explaining, "There are a lot of gas station robberies these days out here in the sticks. I see you have a camera up there, at least you have that. That at least helps us catch the bastards;" he said gesticulating at the camera in the corner of the store.

Bonsai nodded sheepishly, knowing that the camera hadn't been used in years. It had been a long time since he had stopped paying the security company that owned the hardware their monthly subscription fees.

As Bonsai's thoughts had drifted into his lack of payment of utility bills, he had forgotten that the cop was still apparently talking;

"But no, sir," he said with the authority of a civil rights activist, "we are out there too and just a call away if you need us".

Bonsai smiled mechanically and whispered through his lips, "Why thank you, sir. That is comforting".

That is some return on a stale coffee and stinking donut, Bonsai thought sarcastically as he thought about the dollar or two he had made from that particular visitor. Namely, a security service of sorts.

"Well, I'll be getting going. I have highway duties now," the cop added without being asked and then adding sheepishly as if recalling a look of pity from his wife that morning over breakfast and now seeking approval from a gas station worker he didn't know; "A lot of folks are not fans of highway petrol, but it's important work. It saves lives you know," he added rhetorically but maybe half hoping the gas station worker would agree.

Bonsai thought of the Officer sitting in his station on Highway One, perched in his wagon, like a bird of prey.

Sports car after sports car flying past at speed on the Highway below.

Many of the folks headed south for the weekend from San Francisco to Pebble Beach for a golf game or a spa retreat in Big Sur. Those racers were the kind of folks who sported various "Foundation" registration plates to demonstrate their donations to benevolent causes. Donations that, Bonsai, thought cynically, were not so much paid out of philanthropy but more likely with the hopes of ghosting out of parking and speeding tickets or other inconvenient misdemeanors.

No, sir, they wouldn't be getting any speeding tickets or otherwise but maybe for some their day would be inconvenienced by being pulled over in their haste to get to their tee-off time.

Instead, the Ferraris and Porsches (you get the idea) would pass at speed as the Officer ate his sticky pink donut and drank piss weak day old coffee, at least today. And regardless the officer would be happy as a pig in the mud and convince himself he was somehow a man of virtue for sitting on his perch through the duration of his watch.

Bonsai

Bonsai watched the police car kick up dust and head back onto the Highway. He couldn't face any more ghoulish visitors this afternoon, least of all a bunch of thieving teenagers. Moreover, he had other plans to attend too. So, he turned the shop sign to mark the establishment "Closed" and hastily lowered the blinds in the store windows so that soon his station looked like it was the house on the block at Halloween with nobody in it. The house that looked the scariest to kids and kept them away. In other words, it looked haunted, ghostlike. And a whip of dust, blew past the tanks outside to make the point.

As I say, Bonsai needed some respite. He stopped first at the restroom, to the side of the counter, which, of course, had an "out of order" sign on the front. No transient bums had a chance of shitting in his can, did they? He opened the closet with a key attached to his waistband by a sort of climber's belay.

Once inside, a lonely light bulb lit up the room and gave the room the effect that it was a theater performer's changing room. There were little lightbulbs, maybe six or so, either side of the mirror and when they were lit it looked like an actor's dressing room.

In the very real world, Bonsai was an actor of sorts. By which, I mean that inside Bonsai, there were various versions of him. He was a living Russian doll of sorts. You will discover the other characters of this man.

Sandy Nicolson

He closed the door, even though the shop was closed, it made him feel like he was in his mother's womb and safe. He turned on the hot water tap and, filled the basin and added some soap sparingly (as if it were a modern-day luxury) from the pump by its side. The bowl was soon almost full and soapy with suds. He removed his t-shirt, which had a "California Golden Bear" logo on it and underneath it in writing that you had to peer to read if you were inclined too. Some customers who attempted it might think they were overdue for an eye test. Either way, it read, "Living the Dream - and you?". Anyway, if not obvious, Bonsai, well he loved the irony of it.

Bonsai took a moment and looked at himself in the mirror above the sink as it gradually began to steam around the edges of the glass. The little actor light bulbs twinkling. Even in the softish light of the room, Bonsai's first thought, as he looked at his image in return, was, "I feel near my expiration date like an old can of produce in the store".

He was nearly fifty five but a life of hard living had taken its toll on Bonsai, emotionally and physically.

The hard-living wasn't running the garage, as much as that entailed long days and significant amounts of manual labor (and presently without much help). No, it was Bonsai's love of a deck of 52 cards (plus jokers) that can fit in the palm of your hand,

Bonsai

something you at least could somehow feel like you could control, that had led to his particular brand of physical decay. He would play until dawn, drink whiskey like water and make out it wasn't making a difference (for years). And missing his daughter, of course (insert broken heart). Nothing will age you like a broken heart, Bonsai would tell you.

On the face of it, it's a simple game really, poker. A game of comparing cards with other players, placing a wager each round and taking a chance on the "river", the name given to the final run of cards that ultimately determines the worth of an individual player's hand. But of course, there is much more to the game, including psychology, math, and, above all, luck. In the absence of anything else of substance in his life, Bonsai loved that game, more than anything. To Bonsai, well, it represented life.

The game had enthralled Bonsai from the first time he played, and the early games played with his Uncle in the garage forecourt.

Bonsai's Uncle had originally immigrated to the United States in his 20s, but we will get to that in more detail in time.

Bonsai was talented at math, it had been noted at elementary school. This was a fact reflected by the fact that he had won the mathematics prize back in Korea, as a kid, years ago.

Sandy Nicolson

His home life took its toll on him, by which we really mean he took a beating every day for even the most minor indiscretion.

Bonsai's father never recovered from the Korean war, the horrors, what he saw. He developed a taste for opium to escape.

When it came to his mother, well he last saw her somewhere around his 11th birthday.

So, with that beginning he was never going to make it as a Senator, short of a miracle, and well, that never happened. Instead, he worked in the local bus station and developed his trade as a mechanic.

His only fond memories of the time in Korea were of the toy autos his Uncle would send from America that he would push around the lonely linoleum floor of his father's one bedroom apartment as a child, which, as he became an adult, subliminally no doubt drew him to automobile maintenance.

But, the Uncle was a bona fide legend for Bonsai. Ultimately, it was his Uncle who enabled Bonsai to immigrate to a new life in California. Much as he was presently down on his luck, emigrating to the USA was still the greatest escape of his life, and all told his life was significantly better for it.

The memory of his Uncle was never far away in the garage. His father's brother was, as I say, this guy's savior, at least at one point. Before the emphysema that ultimately took him away in the winter of 1979, his Uncle had taught him so much (including English). When Bonsai first moved to the US with such excitement in the early 1970's, the garage sparkled in the fields of Central California and back then, trade roared as vast amounts of agricultural produce were distributed by trucks thirsty for gasoline across the USA, which the garage eagerly supplied.

Whilst his Uncle was the father figure he never had, a mentor, Bonsai, in turn was a great mechanic, neither of them were great business men in return. Ultimately, owning a gas station in the 1970s in the US was no easy enterprise. The great headwind of the energy crisis was in full tilt. There were significant oil supply chain shortages, geopolitical tensions and soaring prices that quickly made the garage loss-making. In fact, in some ways, Bonsai's arrival, you might say, saved the earlier closure of the garage, as he was able to at least bring his mechanical skills to help fix those gas-guzzling cars that needed attention and, in so doing, a much-needed extra source of income to keep the enterprise alive.

One problematic skill that his Uncle passed on to Bonsai was how to play card games for money and, most notably, poker. Not long after Bonsai had arrived, the proverbial gambling needle had entered his vein and the opioid of gambling had indelibly left its lifelong mark on him, much like the other kind had left on his father.

Sandy Nicolson

In the years since his Uncle's passing, Bonsai never really left the garage in any significant way. There was always a shadow of his beloved Uncle somewhere in the place. He was a Shakespearean ghost, of sorts, in that garage in Salinas. There wasn't a day that would go past when he wouldn't see his Uncle in the corner of the store like some kind of ghostly character relaying some piece of wisdom to him.

Presently, Bonsai began washing his face slowly, then his neck, his chest and his armpits. As was the ritual, he returned to his face feeling the marks and scars that were hallmarks of a lifetime of "hanging in there" in the underbelly of Salinas. Eventually, he let the water run out and patted himself down with a series of towels like he was in a fancy spa. He then took a key from his waistband and opened the "Trojan" condom dispenser to the right of the basin, which, of course, had an "out of order" sticker clearly marked on it.

Bonsai opened the metal box with the key and inside found his familiar toiletries. The toiletries of a traveling salesman, the toiletries of a single man, the essentials in other words. There were no extraneous items representing some kind of Christmas or Birthday present for the man who has everything, quite the opposite. There was a toothbrush, toothpaste, shaving foam, a brush, a razor in a cup, a no-name brand deodorant and a bottle of old spice eau de toilette. Stacked high behind the toiletries, though, was the real prize or, rather, the spoils of many nights of toil at the tables.

Stacks of Benjamin bills, in neat rows, as neat as a field of artichokes before harvest. The cash represented his life savings, but more than that, this was the means that would one day set him free from the place. At least, that's what he thought. The meager day's takings that Toad and M had dirtied away that day were irrelevant. These neatly stacked bills in thousand-dollar increments were another thing entirely, but all that said, it was still nothing to boast about. Not really, not to give you a false impression. This was the equivalent of playing two weeks in Vegas at the tables versus a 401K plan of a wealthy, 30 year veteran management consultant professional, but it still represented a healthy sum of cash.

He took the bottle of old spice, splashed some of the liquid on his palms, and patted his cheeks. He allowed himself a small smile; "at least for now, the smell of Toad was gone," and likely forever soon.

After washing, Bonsai carefully locked his safe of sorts. Then, to the right, on a simple hanger, was his modest wardrobe. A few boiler suits, slacks and shirts, his golf clothes, and one black suit. The black suit was one of the most expensive things he owned. He hadn't paid for it. A San Francisco tailor friend of his Uncle had produced it as a favor, and if you looked down at the floor, you would see a couple of well-worn golf shoes, and then, like a Brat

Pack member, there was his proudest possession, a perfectly polished pair of Crocket and Jones brogues made originally in the 1950's in England. Bonsai knew they were coming out of retirement soon. Since he received "the invitation," he had polished them every night.

Bonsai smiled at the shoes in anticipation and then closed the door to the water closet and returned to the store.

The early evening light was now fading, and the sinking sun struck spears of light through the gaps in the Venetian blinds like police searchlights. Bonsai gathered the spilled cash from the floor and returned it to the register. He suddenly felt a little calmer and in a more contemplative mood. He took a can of beer from the store refrigerator and pulled its catch open and with it, there was a sound like a moment of relief had entered the space.

He paused and looked at the lottery machine glinting in that early evening sun by the door. The ticker tape at the top read, "Mega Millions - 400m…..draw date…..17th April".

He struck a wistful smile as he recalled happier times. The year of 1992, April 17, nearly twenty years to the day, the recall of that day came flooding back and enveloped his senses. It was a completely different time in all kinds of ways. Maybe it was the last time he could remember being happy. A completely different light had filled the room that day. His daughter had bounced around the store on "cloud 9" at this new arrival to their world. This strange machine of promise.

"Daddy, daddy, wow, a lottery machine". Lily pressed all the buttons as if the arrival of the machine was the best present in the world. She was 12 years old then.

He had signed the purchase order sheet for the engineer who had completed setting up the new machine set-up. Apparently, he had the only lottery machine in the entire valley, and the engineer had foretold correctly that his gas station would soon be the most popular gas station for miles around. In the approximately six months it took for all the other gas stations to obtain one, in that time, it was true he had the equivalent of the only television in town at the time of the moon landing. It was kind of ironic that he would ultimately gamble away any extra profit he did, in fact, benefit from at that time.

Once he had installed it, the engineer had turned on the switch, and the machine had obediently lit up like a jukebox. The songs it sang promised to change your life. All the machine asked for were a couple of numbers. Six, to be exact. Some folks would pick those at random, and some would dig deep, searching superstitiously for "lucky" numbers from the past. In those early years, it would fascinate Bonsai, looking across at customers as they searched their minds for the right combination of numbers like they were trying to pick the numbers to break a safe, sure, good luck.

Folks would often share at the counter, the source of their numbers. It might be a lucky high school football jersey number, the street number of their first home, their loved one's birthday, the hotel room number where they lost their virginity, or the date of graduation. You get the idea. You name it, people had all sorts of systems for selecting their lottery numbers. All of which were sure-fire strategies to win, of course.

"I think your daughter thinks you've won the lottery yourself!" the engineer laughed, observing her cheerfulness.

"It's her birthday today, she's 12," Bonsai had said as if by explanation and adding in search of more logic, "As you know, if someone buys the winning ticket here, I told her that, the owner of the store, you know us, I mean me, wins a million dollars and of course, she is certain someone will buy the winning ticket here.".

"They will, Daddy." she enthused.

"Well, why don't you buy her a ticket? She can have the first ticket from the machine. But of course, she is too young, so it would be your ticket if you win, of course." He added with a complicit wink.

"I can't buy a ticket, as I own the garage," and adding defensively, "You know that?" as if he was being tested by the

Bonsai

company. Then, adding to lighten his tone, "No, as I say, the hope I have of winning is if someone buys a ticket from the machine and then I get a million! a sort of double serendipity if you think about it".

"Well, let me buy a ticket for her, of course." The engineer said with a benevolent smile.

"That would be pretty cool," Bonsai agreed and instructed his daughter, Lilly, to come over to the machine.

Bonsai offered a dollar from his tip jar, and the engineer waved it away.

"The lottery man here is going to let you be the first ticket owner!"

"Wow," Lily giggled gleefully, "does that mean I win?"

"Unfortunately, that part is not guaranteed," said the Lottery man; "But you have a chance. Everyone has a chance to win," he went on, as if he was in some kind of television commercial, then explaining, "This is how it works, you need to choose 5 numbers and a bonus number. Those numbers may change over time. You can either choose numbers that are completely random up to the number 45, or if you're like me, you pick numbers that signify something. You don't need to tell anyone what they mean, I don't, but I think it's good luck if you keep that secret!"

Sandy Nicolson

"Wow, I want to choose my numbers," replied Lily, looking at her Dad. She followed the engineer's instructions, listening to every word intently. He helped her punch the ticket into the machine, followed by inserting the dollar bill. The machine, in due course, ingested the ticket. A couple of lights blinked, orange, yellow and red, and there was suddenly fairground carousel tune, and in short order, a ticket was released from the beast's belly, like it had just given birth to a dream, and as if by magic, it neatly displayed the numbers that had been chosen.

The engineer handed Lily the ticket. Her Dad now had his hands on her shoulders. She had looked at the ticket and then at both of them in awe. Finally, she had said, looking at her humble paper receipt like it was a letter from the President.

"Dad, this is the best birthday present ever!"

His daughter would be 30 now, and she had left Salinas and ran a long time ago. In fact, today was her birthday. Of course, they hadn't won the lottery that day. She didn't leave school, though, like him at 15, either. In fact, she had gone all the way. She won a different kind of lottery and secured a scholarship at Stanford to read law.

It was on her graduation from High School that they had lost touch. A typical argument about his lack of empathy. In reality he had lost her long before that time. Maybe not winning the lottery

Bonsai

that week finally brought it home to Lily that fairytales don't come true and, most importantly, that she would never see her mother never mind become an instant millionaire. More than that, though, the lottery machine represented the bigger lie, that her father knew what happened to her mother and was never going to tell her. For that, she grew to hate him, and the dream of escaping him, the gas station, and Salinas spurred her on to be as academically successful as she was. At least, that was something she could control.

Bonsai took a slug of his beer as he took stock of the memories and recalled the lost days of innocence with Lily.

Bonsai opened the door to the garage. It was connected by a door behind the cash register. It wasn't deliberate, but the way the cigarette display case hung to the door's side always made it feel to Bonsai when he opened the door that he was entering a secret passage. It was a passage to his space. His enclave, it felt like that to him, anyway. In contrast to the relative communal hell of the store, it was his space to think.

A white 2002 Nissan Camry sat on the ramp. A new muffler needed to be fitted. The old Japanese car hung there, suspended on the ramp, like a piece of institutional art. The owner was a retired Army Captain that Bonsai played golf with, Captain Montgomery (Bonsai called him "Captain"). He was a good man and one of the few (somewhat local) folks Bonsai could call a friend.

Sandy Nicolson

Montgomery had fought in the Korean War back in the 50s and was his Uncle's age (maybe he was the surrogate Uncle to Bonsai since the natural one's passing). In return, Bonsai got the impression Montgomery thought Bonsai was one of the refugees that he had saved in Korea as a US Marine and he thought he was somehow inspired to take care of Bonsai. Some relationships are strange, Bonsai thought.

Their initial meeting had been a simple one. Bonsai had been playing Pacific Grove golf course on a summer's night as a single player and got caught behind some tourists who wouldn't do the honorable thing and let him play through. Montgomery had been playing on his own behind him. As they waited on the tee box, Bonsai had asked him to join him. They became fast friends ever since that round.

"Tourist, huh;" Montgomery had groaned. Bonsai recognized him instantly as a fellow curmudgeon and consequently and instantly knew that they would get along just fine. Despite the beauty of the setting and the perfect sunset over the Pacific Ocean, Montgomery and Bonsai were sort of oblivious to it all. Rather, you could say they were both numb to the natural beauty that surrounded them. Not that they had seen it all before, but rather, they were busy looking inward at their respective demons.

The rest of that first round, Montgomery had cursed each

swing and chain smoked his way around the remaining holes. When Montgomery asked Bonsai, the next time they played, this time at another Bayonet (a course a military heritage and hence the Captain's favorite), Bayonet if he wanted to make the game interesting and play for some "green", Bonsai had simply given a smile that said; "of course" That was such a signature of their relationship, body language, grunts and nods, like they were pseudo clairvoyant and could read each other's minds. Bonsai never asked, but wondered if that was a skill his friend had picked up in the army. He imagined him on tours in countries like Korea where he didn't otherwise speak the local language and instead relied on other, non-verbal, means of communication with the locals to make his commands and communicate with the locals.

The Captain was a; "we are all the same aren't we" kind of guy. He had toured three continents and half a dozen different countries and had come to the conclusion that human beings were pretty much the same miserable bunch the world over.

Bonsai took a seat in his rocking chair in the garage draped in a faded stars and stripes rug. Beside him was his desk. A dirty old PC and printer sat on it. That computer's only function in life was to produce his customers' receipts. Surrounding the old machine were the trophies celebrating what Bonsai really lived for. In number three spot behind, his horticultural love for which he had acquired his moniker, there were approximately 10 or 12 Bonsai trees, 3 of which were over 20 years old, though two had just been potted a week or so ago. In other words, grooming them had been a passion for him for some time.

It wasn't lost on Bonsai in his shabby garage that thousands of years ago, the presence of such miniature trees in the homes of the Chinese lords were symbols of great success and wealth. Sort of ironic if you thought of their estates and his gas station in comparison. These particular trees had truly lucked out, in a sense.

The opulence of a Chinese dynasty versus his humble surroundings wasn't lost on him. He hoped the trees didn't hold it against him. His shabby armchair framed the corner of a space that could only ever be drawn in pen and ink. It was the working room of a gas station off a nondescript anterior road belonging to Highway One near Salinas and it belonged to Bonsai.

If you check Wikipedia, Salinas is an agricultural town in California whose heyday, arguably, was some three hundred years ago. No offense to Salinas folks, it is a great place, but I am just telling you this particular story from Bonsai's perspective!

It's actually true, in fact, that Bonsai was Emperor of his tiny part Salinas.

Amongst his namesake trees, as if she was actually one of

Bonsai

them, was a wooden framed photograph of Lily. She looked identical to his wife, whom he had met at precisely the age of her photograph. It was her graduation photograph. She wasn't much older than the age of most of the miniature trees that surrounded her now on that desk.

In the photographic pose, she wore a slim Mona Lisa smile that spoke, of course, to the childhood trauma of losing her mother prematurely or rather by prematurely meaning, she never knew her.

Her eyes were chestnut brown. They had a haunting, ephemeral feel, if you peered. Her hair was cut in a non-fuzzy, business-like bob. A hairstyle she had her entire life. If you were curious, it told you she was more interested in academia than fashion or similar frivolous interests. She didn't have the luxury of the interests of a typical teenager. Her eyebrows pinched in the middle, giving the impression of a perpetual frown. For the little vanity she had (and on the photographer's insistence), for this rare occasion, she had removed her glasses for the photograph.

To Bonsai, his daughter was the most beloved of all of his trees. Whilst he had not seen her for over a decade, he knew she had blossomed into an even more beautiful lady. The reason he knew, in part, was framed on the wall behind this particular mini forest, a framed edition of the San Francisco Chronicle, with a picture of her in an immaculate trouser suit, announcing her arrival at a prestigious law firm in the city as their youngest ever Partner.

Other symbols of Bonsai's pride, paled in comparison, including a poster of the Korean baseball team, the Haitai Tigers, representing their winning teams in 1983, 1986, 1987, 1988, and 1989. All games came after he left and so he had to follow the games by way of the Korean Baseball publication he had delivered, which usually came two weeks after a game if he was lucky. He had long since adopted the San Francisco Giants as his surrogate team.

Bonsai took a final slug of his beer, rose to his feet, and announced, "How rude of me, ladies. I must offer you a drink". If you listened carefully, his voice was affected, like an English aristocrat as clumsily portrayed in a US-made television movie. He often liked to amuse himself and stave off loneliness by making up voices and characters.

He proceeded to turn on an old radio and the room immediately filled with a Bay Area Jazz station; Miles Davis, Kind of Blue was halfway through.

He then carefully filled a small watering can from a faucet by the garage door and treated each plant to a precise drizzle (you have to be careful not to overwater a Bonsai). He had the precision of a sommelier in a high-class hotel. He carefully administered the perfect pour. This was an evening ritual we are getting a peek at. He took his time to take in the beauty of his daughter in the soft early evening light that filled the room, a light that was unique to that part of the world. Tonight, she looked more beautiful than ever. For 30 years of her life, it had felt surreal to Bonsai that she had been, at least in part, created by him, just like his beloved trees. The partner of that creation was not represented on the desk, of course (there is a reason for that, which we will get to). Like his daughter, she had gone from his life as quickly as she had entered it. Bonsai didn't need a picture to remember either her beauty or the pain her memory created for him with her vanishing. He had to suffer that pain every time he looked at Lily's face.

As Bonsai followed his evening ritual, Lily, of course, was still alive, even in the picture form in front of him. He knew she hated him. He understood why. He knew that was principally for not telling her about her mother, but of course, he couldn't. Other than a few vacuous comments like she was "beautiful," just like her, he had never shared her identity or anything material about her. In reality, though, of course, Bonsai knew who she was, but in a way, he didn't actually know that much more than Lily. But he did know he loved them both still.

Sandy Nicolson

Chapter 3

Let's Meet Lily In Person

It was, and yet it wasn't a long way from Salinas. In one way, Salinas is only 110 miles or so from San Francisco, but it felt to me like a different universe, far, far away from my life as a child. That feeling seemed to be especially acute now that I had a new life that could not be more remote to the one I had growing up.

I lived and worked in San Francisco as a corporate lawyer. I had the so-called privilege of working for some of the biggest technology companies in the world. It was hard to say if, from a corporate or personal perspective, I had met what folks back home would call "good" people in this new world. I say that as someone who was brought up in the countryside. Salinas is not the Midwest, but from a California perspective, it might as well be. Back home, the majority of people go to Church on Sundays, vote Republican, eat pie and know their neighbors. In San Francisco, everything is the opposite, especially knowing your neighbor's part. Candidly, I couldn't say one way or another, aside from my girlfriend, her family and my work colleagues, I hardly knew anyone in San Francisco, and part of that was because of my job, but also, part of it was deliberate. I enjoyed the anonymity. I enjoyed not having to know someone else's business and pass judgment on it or feel they were passing judgment on me. Most importantly, I enjoyed people

Bonsai

not asking questions about me. You could say I was a bit of a loner, but for my relationship with my girlfriend, that is.

Here we are in 2010, and it's the so-called second coming, so to speak, for Tech after the "dot com" crash ten years ago. Bear with me because I am self-aware enough to know that folks like me in the tech world, in Silicon Valley, live, well, in a bit of a bubble. And so, I will try and not use vernacular such that I lose you.

For the most part, my clients were software engineers by profession (number crunchers or aka robots in some cases if someone like me was being cruel or at least folks that were obsessed with computer code). Alpha males for the most part, amazing at coding but typically not so great at empathy or interpretative skills, emotional intelligence, communication, etc., and so, that's how I found my niche by filling that void for them. In a nutshell, that is what made me so successful. Sort of ironic that I was naturally an introvert in my personal life but so extraverted at work. I know someone would say you can be an introvert and be outgoing, too, but that's too complicated for me to give you the picture here, and I confess to not really understanding it either.

If you captured my job description as a corporate lawyer, it would be writing customer and supplier contracts and all that entails, negotiating with everyone that the company needed me too, helping hire their employees, defending and protecting their fledgling products/their so-called "secret sauce". To put it succinctly, I did their talking. I did their bidding for them, I was their representative. I wouldn't say, you know, I made them successful, but at the same time, I was, you know, significantly helpful, and without me, it is fair to say, they wouldn't be as successful as they were.

My colleagues in my boutique law firm were different from me in terms of their backgrounds. Simply put, they came from rich families. They were not the daughter of a failed gas station owner in Salinas. But that suited me just fine, I was hungrier, more hard-boiled, you might say, than them as a result, more driven, you could say. How many of them could change a carburetor of a 1975 Ford Mustang and at the same time know whether a data privacy contract clause had been breached? Well, you know me, that's who.

The more they talked about their childhoods filled with stories of private schools, pool parties in Atherton, pony riding in Woodside, winter holidays skiing in Vail, or summers in Provence or Tuscany at a friend's holiday home, quite frankly, the more it drove me to work harder and be the best at what I did and most importantly, better than them.

As a result of my industry, I was in sync with the robots who worked all night to create their techno toys. I mean, I shared their work ethic. Few of them even knew Salinas existed, and I am talking about folks who have lived in the Bay their whole lives. No, they

Bonsai

likely couldn't pin it on the map if they had to. A strange thing in a way.

On the day of my thirtieth birthday, I had woken very early as usual, around 5 am, as a function of life in the gas station, where I would help my dad unpack boxes of quick noodles and candy and restock the store before it opened every day. As I grew older, I just never reset my personal alarm clock. I woke up right on time to get the store ready, in other words.

I kissed my girlfriend on the cheek, and she mumbled, "Happy birthday honey, see you tonight!"

And with that, I was gone into the darkness of the Mission district in San Francisco, where I had my apartment. I loved entering the Mission at that time in the morning, there was still a hive of activity from the night before, street crawlers, peddlers and drunks that had all still to raise their white flags and call it a night or day. Night before? I don't think the Egyptian calendar, to be honest, made a difference to these folks.

By lunch, I had spoken to colleagues in Europe and India and redrafted a bunch of contracts; clauses, terms and conditions, warranties and indemnities, anyway I won't bore you with legalese.

By 12 o'clock, somewhat predictably, my team was knocking on the glass of my hip designed architectural office wall.

They all held pink balloons, each marked with "30" and I could see one of the juniors was holding a tray of cupcakes with pink gooey icing.

I had already forgotten it was my birthday, until they knocked.

"Surprise!" they mouthed through the glass, and, to my horror, as if on cue, like a door-to-door seller when you open your front door, they entered into a discordant obligatory sing-song of "Happy Birthday".

"Hoorah, how lucky am I?" I thought snidely.

The client lunch my EA had in my schedule, turned out to be a surprise birthday celebration at a Dim Sum restaurant near the office with my team. In truth, I really needed this like a hole in the head. I had so much to do, and if I didn't get home to Lauren for our dinner on time, I knew we would fight.

We both had been ships in the night over the last few months. We seldom fought, but when we did, it was typically to do with my schedule and my prioritizing a work meeting or call over one of our dates that she had planned. So, I was as polite as I could be, but as soon as I realized I had served enough time with folks celebrating my birthday, I gave an excuse to leave. After all, this was lunch with a boss (me) they would rather not be having anyway. I was sure of that.

Bonsai

There were theatrical attempts for me to stay longer. But I said thank you and told them sincerely, I really must return for an important client call but thanks again for all of this, "No, really, what a surprise! No, really, it has been so wonderful," I assured them unconvincingly.

When we returned to the office, my Executive Assistant tugged my arm and said, like a private detective at the end of a show, "Just one thing, Lily," and handed me an opened envelope.

I knew the scrawl of handwriting on the front of the envelope instantly and, therefore knew, who it was from. Bonsai, my dad.

Ever since I left Salinas, somehow, this same envelope would get to me on my birthday. It was our ritual forever, after all. Albeit this ritual was born out of happier times in my early childhood. Well, I am not 100 percent sure that's true, but I will say that to contribute to the story. It was a time when I believed in miracles, like believing we would actually win the lottery and escape from the smell of gasoline. A time when I still believed I would meet my mother again. A dream that never happened.

I knew what was inside the envelope. I brushed off the intrigue or, rather, my EA's prying nature.

"Why would someone send you a lottery ticket with no comment?" she asked, prying. I was probably being too sensitive, as

I don't think she was that observant, but I was self-conscious that she stared at me a lingering stare, maybe seeing me unusually vulnerable.

I wanted to tell her, "It's none of your business:" but I smiled instead, which likely annoyed her more. She was one of the older admins that my firm kept. These Admins, for the most part, only kept their jobs out of the nostalgia of the older Partners who had started their career with them and no doubt, in some cases, were managing the risk of affairs they had with them or were having with them. So those particular admins had jobs for life, and as they say in corporate speak, "they had leverage". Those admins usually were worse than rich housewives; they, in reality, didn't have to work and were guaranteed a revenue stream. At any rate, all this was compounded by the California labor laws that made it impossible to fire them either way. In my case, this was just another example for her to chalk up over dinner with her husband, an example of my peculiarity.

"She got a lottery ticket in an envelope today. How weird is that?,... You want some parmesan cheese with that?" I could hear her say.

Like every year, it was just a simple ticket with a set of numbers that hadn't changed since I was seven, except one that did change, my age, and so, the number 30 he had chosen as this year's

Bonsai

bonus ball. Predictable, Bonsai.

Miraculously, I managed to leave the office (somewhat) on time. I fought off some of the team trying to convince me we needed to go for a happy hour. I promised them instead that we would do something at the end of the week. So, I managed to escape and stepped out into the freedom of Market Street and the instant obscurity that came from being immediately surrounded by a throng of tourists, homeless folks, and, you know, most importantly, nobody I knew. I instantly felt I could breathe again. I took big gulps of polluted air to meditate on and it was just what I needed to find some sense of serenity.

I decided I yearned for a little time with some strangers for company, and so rather than take an Uber home, I took the Muni. It was a far safer option than having a taxi driver disturb my meditative intent with meaningless small talk. Anyway, that's what I thought, and before you judge me, it was my birthday.

I took a seat next to a guy who looked like he had been on the bus all day and was only now partially waking up. It was 6 pm, and it was 2010, and for all we knew, this guy just a few years ago could have been a successful investment banker, such are the margins in life, you could go from a high to low point so quickly, I knew that from my Dad of course. The filthy Burberry overcoat was either a good find in a Goodwill basket or something he bought in better times.

Sandy Nicolson

I felt a little privileged that I was maybe one of the few people, at least in my firm, who realized the margins in life were really that small. It wasn't a Hollywood thing, it was real. I had that perspective.

Who knew what this guy's story was, but it just took one or two wrong turns after the subprime housing market collapse for many people to end up on this bus, really with nowhere to go, stinking of yesterday's piss. I pitied them.

It fascinated me that there were people who had been enjoying a relatively comfortable life working for an investment bank before the crash happened. I am not talking about the traders but the support folks, the back office. They had comfortable lives but still had mortgages, healthcare, and kids to take care of. Unlike the traders, they didn't have large investment accounts of their own to fall back on. Then, the crash happened. They defaulted on their own mortgage as a result. Maybe their marriage fell apart under the tension that followed the disruption (I made that up, who knows!). Maybe they took an opioid or two to pretend it wasn't happening. It was no surprise to me that the opioid crisis practically happened at the same time. The pursuit of a numb state was all some folks could hope for. Before you know it, that smart-suited person who left their house once upon a time with a purpose became this semi-permanent resident of Muni. You know, presently sitting next to me.

Bonsai

But those stories were different from mine. I had never known wealth before I moved to San Francisco. I had never sat at the front of a plane, eaten in a restaurant that had silverware or had someone that took my order, I never bought clothes that I may or may not wear. So, I had nothing to miss if it went wrong. I don't know if you really understand that, maybe some do. These folks didn't have that experience of, well, having nothing, really nothing, to contrast with and I think that is why it hurt them so bad.

That financial crisis was the first time in a generation that the middle class had such a disruptive experience that way. A glimpse, at least for them, of hell on earth. Am I exaggerating? Hmm, I don't actually think so.

The resident of hell presently looked at me with one eye suspiciously. He looked like he was questioning me for making any assumptions. He looked like he could read my mind, or maybe he was just high, crazy or both. Who knows? And who knows what he thought of me!

A summer rain drizzled down the window beside me, mixing the colors of Market Street's neon store signs beyond. The window instantly looked like some kind of Jackson Pollock.

The evocative scene sort of encapsulated my mood on this birthday milestone. I was confused and at once, somewhat melancholic.

Sandy Nicolson

A memory of my dad came to me. I could picture him listening to some Jazz greats in that seat of his, in his "den",

As a child, I got to know Thelonious Monk, Miles Davis, and Charles Mingus, all of whom talked too loudly on their instruments whilst he worked on cars in his garage. Happy but sad, Sad but happy, they would intonate and sort of create the theme tune of my childhood working in the garage alongside Bonsai.

I looked at the envelope that, for some reason, I was now holding in front of me. Subconsciously, I must have taken it from my handbag and just held it there in front of me. Sort of staring at it, can you believe it?

I thought, 30 years old, huh? Some things change, some don't, some do. So, consider yourself lucky if that doesn't resonate!

In fact, maybe this was the winning ticket this year, I thought sarcastically, 30 being the bonus ball, of course. I wasn't sure what I would do, what I would change, you know, in my life, even if by some hapchance, you know I, at last, won. No amount of money would help me find my mother, of course. Gosh, did I bring that up again? Okay, let me come back to that.

The indulgent thoughts made me cringe in recall of my naive 12-year-old self dancing around the store when that original lottery machine was fitted in my dad's store. You know, don't think bad of

Bonsai

me, I think I am a loser romantic, but I had thought it represented the answer to our dreams, an escape from Salinas, from the gas station to somewhere sparkling and shiny. Somewhere we could jump to free of our past, like walking through the wardrobe of a CS Lewis novel I adored at the time. Most of all, I thought it was a ticket to finally meet my mother as if money was what kept us apart.

Alas, I had to have 12 years of calluses on my hands and proverbially on my brain, years of hard work to finally get free of that garage, free of that town, free of him. There were no fairy tales in my childhood, and despite the geography, I wasn't really free of those memories and of the one thing I had always yearned for, my mother. Who simply put, I never knew!

My mind drifted, like in one of those jazz records you know my Dad loved, abstractly to the team lunch earlier that day. I smirked. What a forced affair it had been, a team-building exercise packaged as a family affair. The family part was truly artificial, of course. There had been a recent drive by HR, no doubt driven by the Harvard Business School management theory of the day, that by creating a "family" culture, the team would work more cohesively, more effectively and ultimately more profitably for the Partners. Or so our Managing Partner and a faceless management consultant had presented at our Town Hall.

The launch of "Project Family", the slide behind them read

on the stage, as the strategy had been announced to us all.

The Managing Partner, a short, bespeckled New Yorker, conveyed his portion of the talk awkwardly and, thus, further undermining its sincerity. The management consultant sensed it and like a frustrated band member who thought his other band member had not hit the right notes, he quickly took over the mic. Alpha personalities, I thought. They both wanted to lead.

The management consultant then hit us up with his proverbial guitar solo. He talked over the Managing Partner, announcing stridently that it was critical that we ensure our employees truly know they are "loved". We were told to close our eyes and remember someone who had truly loved us and remember, more than that, how that felt. "Please, you know, let's take a moment," he had said!

That was the feeling our employees must feel. A feeling of warmth, a sense of value, a sense of belonging. Instill that feeling in a member of staff, and they would never want to leave our firm and if they did, they would miss us, the way you miss your family, your loved ones. I had thought of my Dad, Bonsai, of course, him and I playing poker and arguing over whether the cards had been adequately shuffled. Really? Did you? Yes, let's just play, please.

Both of us with our sullen poker faces, him unable to show the hurt he felt inside and my inability to show him I cared about him. God, help my team, I thought. It felt artificial and contrived, sinister even. I didn't buy into the idea, but paradoxically I realized at the same time I felt envious of the happy-clappy faces around me in the auditorium, nodding and lapping up every word. "Let's love each other, you, your team, the firm!!" Hoorah. Really?

I shared my cynicism on the whole thing with Lauren one night over dinner. I doubted, probably too harshly, that either of these men had ever truly loved anyone in their lives apart from themselves and maybe money. But of course, hypocritically, to my fellow Partners, I told them how much I loved every bit of it. "Sure, that was magnificent, no really. It was truly inspiring!".

It made me think of my own family's dysfunctionality, of course. I hadn't seen my father in nearly a decade, and my mom, of course, I had never met. I smiled sardonically as I thought of loving my work colleagues and concluded, with some comfort, that the reality of those management theory textbooks was that actually the corporate "family" wasn't any less dysfunctional than the real version.

This train of thought made me confirm to myself that my team really didn't want to be with me earlier eating birthday cake, like a bunch of children at a twelve-year-old's party, rather than the adult lawyers they were. In particular, the manager who presented me with the cakes with a smirk summed it all up, you know, not soundtrack, usually Bruce Springsteen, still playing on the stereo. She couldn't have been more irritating and called me "kid" all the time, and in return, I called her "cliche". She was so dumb she probably didn't even know what that word meant. Well, thinking that kept me sane.

Thankfully, though, disaster struck for her inevitably, I suppose. Her "iceberg hits the Titanic" moment was when she stole my dad's money. I knew my Dad well enough, you never steal a gambler's money. It is like hiding any addicts' drugs!

He had been playing cards until the small hours on his usual Friday night routine. I had the horror of having to watch a Vietnam War movie that she thought would bond us and at the same time watch her eat pickled sardines from a jar. She slurped each one of them whole like a seal. Of course, my dad passed out as soon as he was home. When he woke at 4 am to open the store, she was gone, and so too was his $5,000 winnings that he uncharacteristically hadn't locked up in the condom safe he thought I didn't know about.

When it was apparent a month later that she was never coming back, I was cruel and hounded him by saying mean things like, "That is what love will do to a man". Obviously, I didn't really know what I was talking about, at least on the love front, but I was secretly happy that our strange normality was restored and of course, the apartment was spotless again.

being mean. I had actually surprised her earlier in her performance review (to me, it was no surprise, her work was awful) by telling her that her performance wasn't good enough. She hadn't taken it well and stared at me passive-aggressively, like in her mind's eye, she was planning my killing in the most brutal of ways. As she left my room, she looked like she wanted to cry but didn't want me to have the satisfaction of seeing that I had brought it out in her.

You couldn't blame them for not wanting to be there, for not loving me. After all, I was known for my blunt style and my unrealistic expectations of long-fee earnings hours. My nickname was the "light," but not in a positive sense, but rather I had been given the name on account of the light in my room being on 24/7 as I was always there. "No life;" is what they likely said about me in the bars after work or to their other halves over supper.

It was true. I wasn't charming either, at least to the team. What infuriated many of them was that I was charming to my clients. For clients, of course, I laid the charm on thick. Sure, if I needed to, I would flirt with them. This chameleon-like nature I had only served to compound my team's hatred of me. It rightly built a perception that I wasn't authentic either to them or really to the clients. Most people suspected I was really in it for the money, but if it were just that, at least there would be an honesty to it, so actually, no, there must be something more twisted to my

Bonsai

motivations. This was all conjecture at the end of the day, but nevertheless, I was convinced it was true.

What was my paltry defense for my bad behavior, to myself, if I needed one? I am an out-of-towner! I wasn't afforded the privilege of nepotism. I had to work hard and without a leg up. Secondly and candidly, for all my ability to interpret a legal contract and the English meaning the words within it should or should not convey, I wasn't blessed with the ability for "title tattle". In that regard, I will admit it, I was like my father. In other words, again, introverted. Sure, that's right, I had a poker face, if you want to go there.

I had learned a fair bit of what I would call the "soft furnishing" conversations of the local elite topics. The extraneous stuff, to me anyway. Like where it was fashionable to ski, what sports team was doing well, the best Michelin star restaurants in the city of the day, who was currently playing at Symphony Hall, a critique of the Pulitzer prize-winning novel they had just read. I was, of course, scared to engage in those topics. For if I did, I feared those people would see me as not authentic, a phony and at worst, see me as just the girl from the gas station in Salinas counting out their change and not worthy to be amongst them. After all, this was precisely the quality that made me so successful with my clients, the robots, "I could get to the point quickly". In reality, of course, the other Partners could see through the fact that I was not one of them, but they also knew I was a brilliant lawyer. That was good enough for me.

When it came to my clients, most of whom were dominated by male leadership and founders, there was no room for corporate love, not even a fake corporate love hug, if you will. Most of those clients couldn't give a shit about my so-called "soft furnishings". My success has proven that. I would go further and say that my matter-of-fact appearance was an advantage with these types. There were no distractions, nothing superlative, either looks or small chat. Instead, they listened to my economic use of language and marveled as I cut straight to the point and succinctly told them what to do with confidence.

"Do we have a deal, Lily? Yes or No?" the client would usually ask at the end of one of my negotiations. They couldn't care less about the details or, moreover, what I was going to do over the weekend if, in fact, I had any spare time from assembling their contracts to do anything other than laundry.

For a moment, I wondered whether escaping Salinas and the associated memories of searching for my mother was the only reason I had worked so hard. I heard a stanza of an old Miles Davis tune, a favorite of my dad's, in my head that in words said bitter-sweetly, "Who knows? You may never".

Bonsai

Then I thought of Lauren waiting for me. My girlfriend. My one and only true love. An interior designer from Palo Alto. Blonde tousled hair, big brown eyes. I did love her, didn't I? I questioned myself. Wow, all the cliches of questioning yourself at 30 years old were maybe true.

Unlike so many other fathers, and indeed hers, my father showed no emotion whatsoever when he caught me kissing my first girlfriend in high school. She just happened to be a redheaded girl called Tamara in the year below whom I was ostensibly coaching math too. It was in our tiny apartment above the garage, that we would do our sessions, math tutorials, that is, and I was so embarrassed that it was so modest. So modest, that I really don't want to describe it to you, that's how much it embarrasses me!

Anyhow, one day the doorway sprung open unexpectedly and the key point is not the spartan décor of the room, but that all he said, matter of fact, was, "Don't forget we need to be up early in the morning. You should call it a day soon". That was it and he never spoke about it.

My Dad never asked me one question about my sexuality. I didn't know whether to be exasperated that even that couldn't tease an emotion from him. Did he just accept me, love me no matter what? Or did he just not care? The shoulder shrug and poker face were as usual all that I got in return from my probing.

Sandy Nicolson

My math girl made a tremendous fuss, on the other hand, when her parents found out about us. She pleaded that I never tell anyone in class and that if I did, she would tell everyone that I molested her, and everyone would believe her, as my family was so weird anyway, she explained. So, that was my one and only high school fling, I don't think you could call it a girlfriend, but following that I was celibate for the remainder of High School.

The only thing my dad said, in relation to my sexuality, was a sarcastic joke as we unloaded a box of condoms in the store a week later; "well, you won't be needing these, Lily". "Funny dad!"......and of course, he got a atypical "poker face" reaction from me.

Unlike me, my girlfriend, Lauren, was the product of generations of good breeding. Maybe that is why we were attracted to each other. Opposites attract is the old cliche.

One of her friends joked that if we were dogs, I would be the Rottweiler, and she would be the labrador. Maybe mongrel, for me, would be more accurate if you are making a fair social class comparison.

We have only been together for two years, but our love you could say is unconditional, at least I think it is. Is it? Do you think it's wrong to even question that? I am her first and only lover (at least, that is what she told me after we first made love). But despite all of that, I am still racked with such insecurity. Questions about

Bonsai

our relationship constantly swirl in my head. Am I missing something? Am I?

Why did she love me?

Was it simply that I was her first, and she was too scared to have tried to meet someone else?

Was it my dominant style that she loved?

Was it that she really knew I came from the other side of the tracks that gave her kicks?

Did she pity me, and I hadn't noticed?

Was it because I was a lawyer?

Did the fact I made it to the top in such an alpha male environment turn her on?

It was so ironic that in every other aspect of my life, I had total confidence, but yet these types of questions continued perpetually in my head.

It was when I was in this train of thought I ultimately worried whether I really knew her at all.

In pursuit of the GPA, (I needed to get into Stanford and, with it, an escape ticket from Salinas and my father), I had worked through most nights and volunteered for anything I could. That work ethic had continued into to my current profession, and I knew Lauren hated it e.g. she wanted to see me more.

She almost never read though. I mean Lauren never read literature. It was one of my bugbears. Currently, I was trying to get her to read East of Eden. Steinbeck right?

Salinas, through a different lens, I suppose. So, I asked Lauren to read it and you know, I pleaded with her, in my apartment, to read it. But she didn't.

If you have read it, for me, it's one of the books that brings great beauty to Salinas and speaks to the toughness and resilience of the people who live off the land. In short, it was my subliminal way of trying to get Lauren to better understand me. I was going to drive her down to meet my estranged father in the Gas Station after all. Not now, but you know, maybe one day. I struggle to even picture what that would look like right now. I haven't even seen him in such a long time.

I can't tell you how many times I have read that book and fantasized that the mother who was absent from her children's lives and (spoiler alert) ran a whore house in say "East of Eden;" might just, I mean, who knows, but might just be like my own mother out there somewhere doing something illicit. "I forgive you! really I do," I would howl, crying myself to sleep.

Bonsai

Maybe that was why she had abandoned me, you know. At least there was some logic to that, I hope you understand and forgive me for being so presumptive and maybe even self-indulgent.

When I was growing up, every Asian woman I ever saw in the 40-60 year old age bracket (even on television), I would study their face, their mannerisms, and maybe, their gait.

Could they be the one?

Could that be her?

Was that my mother?

I would ask myself these questions constantly.

A melancholy would sweep over me whenever I thought of my mother. Birthdays were the worst time for it. The carousel of questions that would run through my head, like as I speak to you now, are always the same;

Why did she leave me?

What did she look like?

Did she look like me?

What would she sound like to me? If I met her, at least?

What did she smell like?

Would she instantly love me if she met me?

Sandy Nicolson

Unconditionally.

Would she cry when we met?

Would she love me for who I am in all senses?

What did I mean by that?

Would she know instinctively?

And today, would she remember it's my birthday?

I could go on and on…..with these questions……

I stopped asking my father about my mother sometime before I became a teenager. That didn't mean I stopped thinking about her every day, often to distraction, though.

Just to be clear, I exhausted every approach with my Dad. I literally tried everything. I was emotional and pleaded with him (in so many ways). I am not ashamed to say I beat him. I had blackmailed him. I had run away and hid for a week in the Big Sur. I had ransacked the apartment.

I asked everyone in town about my mother, as soon as I was mature enough to do so and they all looked at me blankly. Everytime, I could tell, they really did not know.

Last year, I hired a private investigator who managed to pull the missing person reports the Police ran when I was born. All my

Bonsai

father had stubbornly said was my mother was simply gone.

I found out in my adult years that a local church had tried to have me put into foster care when I was 2 years old.

At the Children's panel, they had proven by DNA that Bonsai was my father. Many years later, to read that and feel that was life affirming was, well, slightly strange for me.

A critical factor, though in my father keeping custody of me and resisting the challenge of the Church, was the testimony of a lady called Martha.

Martha was a local Mexican grandmother, a well-respected mother of a well-regarded businessman. She had asserted to the hearing that my father was a good man and that she was involved in supporting my upbringing. Her testimony was so compelling that the Court acquiesced in my Father's favor, and he kept custody of me.

Martha actually became a surrogate grandmother until she passed away in my last year at high school. She only ever scolded me once when I told her that I wished I had been given away to another home. She only had to do that scolding once, and for all my continual tactics with my father, I dropped that antic out of respect for her.

Today, I have come to the conclusion that the only person

who knows, who really knows about my mother, who is alive anyway, is Bonsai.

Of course, there were all kinds of fantastical tales in the town growing up about my mother, like;

My mother had died in childbirth or;

She was an illegal immigrant;

She was a Senator's daughter or;

She was an underage girl or;

She had been abducted by aliens....

Or just plain town gossip, like

Bonsai wasn't really the legitimate father;

Bonsai murdered her;

She was an alien!

In short, there was no end to the stories and people's creativity in trying to work out what had happened to Mom. Whoever she was!

The hardest part for me, which I find impossible to admit, most of all to *him*, is that deep down, I do know that my father loves me, and if it wasn't for him, I wouldn't have a roof over my head or food or education and all those things as a child. I am not so cold

Bonsai

that I don't realize that it must have been incredibly difficult for him, and in particular for a man who was the least in touch with his feminine side or any emotional side for that matter that I have known. After some years away, what I realized was that maybe the real reason I left town ultimately wasn't really because of my mother, who I had in reality long since resigned to never seeing, but rather that my father's love was intoxicating and I needed to live, to breathe.

I often wondered if I had known my mother, would that have made a difference? Would she have accepted my sexuality unconditionally the way my father had? I honestly don't know why I worry about that! I think it's just that more generally, you know, I wanted to know her and, in return, for her to love me no matter what.

If my father had given me more than the postage stamp knowledge of my mother, I might have had a clue how she might have felt and given you a fuller picture here.

Instead, all I had to go on was the ultimately unenlightening, maddeningly simple statement, "She was beautiful and smart, just like you." every time I asked, who was she? What was she like? If only, I had known something substantive about her. I had asked everyone in town and then gave up, no one knew who she was. No one.

All they said was that one day, Bonsai was a loner, and the

next, he had a baby girl and that he refused to talk about it. Eventually, people stopped asking. How he had managed to raise a beautiful and smart daughter was beyond them. Anyway, that's what most people said. It was all maddening, really.

My dad had always been a mysterious outsider in our town. Having a child without an obvious partner only served to make it worse and to alienate him even further from the town. Frustratingly, he loved that, and it compounded his introversion. His poker face whenever I argued with him was so infuriating, he showed no emotion, ever.

I went through so many different emotional phases growing up.

Sometimes I just wanted it to be me and my dad versus times when I yearned for a stepmother. You know, someone who would go shopping with me (even though I didn't like shopping), someone who would help me dress, someone who wasn't so incredibly awkward explaining my menstrual cycle, someone who could help me understand relationships, someone who could be there for me and be my friend. I don't even know whether other people have that? You know that type of intimate relationship, with their mother.

There was only one woman, or at least one that I was aware of, that Bonsai had been with in my entire childhood. She was a butch-looking trucker from Los Angeles who made a habit of

Bonsai

stopping at the station on her way North. She had a cringeworthy sense of humor and a laugh that was worse. A real witch-like cackle laugh that I could hear in the store as I did my homework upstairs.

Our relationship really didn't get off to the best start when I caught my dad screwing her in the awful toilet at the back of the store. The kind of place thought that type deserved to be reserved. This was about a week or two after I had noticed her more frequent visits and my dad behaving like a teenager with excitement about the prospect of her visiting again. I was instantly jealous of the intimacy they shared. You're probably nodding, "Sure, of course, you were". Okay, smart ass.

Inevitably, their relationship graduated from the childish storeroom flirting to our apartment and ultimately, she lived with us for about 3 months, maybe longer. I actually can't be exact. I was about 14 years old. Like most kids, I was really awkward at that age at the best of times, let alone having a strange 40-something trucker chick staying with us with her cackle. She was a slob, too. I had always kept our modest apartment in perfect shape. Maybe taking on a motherly role, I am not sure. That cliche makes me cringe. Who knows how that psychology works? But I do know that she joined our tight unit, and she brought a tornado of disruption to it. I would wake to half-eaten takeaways in our sitting room, an empty bottle of whiskey, an overflowing ashtray and the previous evening's

Bonsai

It was probably inevitable that I went through a phase in my teenage years of being incredibly jealous of my classmates who had ostensibly perfect families. I've matured somewhat in my outlook now, but then, exacerbated by the television shows of the time, Full House, The Wonder Years, The Cosbys, and even Rosanne, the unattainable dream was to have a perfect mother and father. I wanted that more than a sibling. When my best friend at 14, Jennifer's parents divorced after her mum ran off with the local preacher, I had to contain my excitement that she was going to be messed up just like me. How sick is that? I zealously gave her advice on how to run the household and, most importantly, get what she wanted from her Dad.

To think, my father didn't even have a photograph of my mother that I could study for clues or share why and how she had left. At least Jennifer knew her mother before she left. I didn't need a therapist (that Lauren introduced me to) to answer in the affirmative that any of the above would have helped me understand my love for Lauren more and, in return, appreciate why she cared for me so much.

I never took much interest growing up in the way I looked. I am not sure if that was a deliberate reaction to not having a mother around or not, but I simply never felt the need to wear a fancy dress or wear makeup, for that matter. I was a real tomboy. Sure, I was teased at school, but after a while, the bullies got bored, mostly because they could never get a rise from me. I knew how to give them a poker face.

I genuinely couldn't care less. My nickname at school was Patty, after the cartoon character Peppermint Patty. Moreover, my father didn't pay much interest in helping me either, so it wasn't uncommon for me to turn up at school with oil on my hands from helping my dad with some car he was fixing wearing dungarees. As I grew older, though, I grew taller and stronger and most of the bullies didn't come near me, I think because mostly they were scared of me or just that I was different.

My girlfriend, on the other hand, was completely the opposite. She had beautiful molten gold blonde hair, the kind of hair that other girls would ask if it was natural and marvel at its beauty like it was a natural wonder and her blue eyes that were disarmingly honest. Her ski body came from an active lifetime of working out, ballet, horse riding, tennis and skiing, I suppose.

The melancholic self-indulgent jazz tune played on in my head ended, and I smiled inwardly at my now 30-something musings being played out in a public bus that was not much different from the one in the opening sequences of the 30-something show that Lauren loved, "Sex in the City". Maybe subconsciously, that is why I chose the muni! I took stock of where we were as we headed

Bonsai

through the Mission, maybe five or so blocks before my stop. I better concentrate, I thought. I often had a bad habit of reviewing work emails on my Blackberry intensely on muni trips home and completely missing my stop as a consequence. In fact, on one occasion, I didn't come up for air until I realized the bus had completed at least one loop and returned to the city where I had started the journey an hour or so before.

Sandy Nicolson

Chapter 4

How Lily Met Lauren

I met Lauren in a bar in Palo Alto 2 years ago. Despite her disarmingly young complexion, she was actually older than me by 2 years. I don't know why that detail matters, but anyway, there you go.

We would joke at parties that we wished we could say we met in an aid project in Africa, but we didn't. We met in a bar in Palo Alto, as I say, which is as symmetrically opposite as that daydream could possibly be.

It was one of those bars of that time that had popped up to serve the employees of booming tech companies. A reclaimed piece of commercial property that had been repossessed in the financial crisis. Ironically, it most likely had been a bank, maybe a Wells Fargo, who knows, the kind of commercial space that whatever filled it still felt completely wasted with incredibly high ceilings and faux Roman murals on the ceilings.

Its refurbishment had filled it with frosted metal, sunken lights, and red leather. It all gave it the impression that it was trying to be cool. Woven through the redesign was an Asian theme. There were mock Buddha statues, water features in every corner, and candles that projected a dark chocolate orange light. The thud of

Bonsai

techno on the sound system greeted you with a volume set so high it was almost impossible to hear what the hostess who greeted you was saying. It was such a contradiction, I thought. The Asian thing was presumably to make connection with an inner Karma, and then, like a defibrillator, the techno brought you right back into the present ghastly reality. In short, it wasn't the most romantic of places to meet the person you fell in love with. I hope you get the picture.

It was all very pretentious. You needed a password to gain entry. You dare not order a cosmopolitan from the mixologist; it would be an insult to them, or so my colleague told me as we entered the bar.

I had just closed a big deal at the firm. My client was a data storage company you would know, which had grown from 10 employees when I first met them a year previously, and it had mushroomed to 500 or so and at that time, they were hiring at a tremendous pace. As was the vogue at the time, they went on an inorganic buying spree and sought to buy any other company that resembled a competitor, which, to the untrained eye, actually provided the exact same product. Maybe you're into it, but data storage? Do you know the difference between one of those companies and the next? Right, I thought so. Apparently, their product was better than the next though, and if they were allowed to continue to be independent, they would eclipse my client, so the natural solution was to acquire them.

For the engineers involved, apparently, the code that they were essentially acquiring, the target's main asset seemingly, was like an exotic mineral from a country most of us had never heard of in a bygone time.

So, the fact we had sealed the deal made a lot of white male software engineers very happy and rich, of course, through the stock options that had lured them to join the company in the first place.

The faux Asian cushions irked me for some reason, maybe I was tired. I took a seat and tried to breathe after what had been a stressful week. I was mentally exhausted. I ran through the head debates I had with my dad as he worked on his cars. What is more stressful? I had probed, you know, as a kid, physical or mental work stress? He hedged his bets frustratingly and said both. I was convinced that mental work was much harder, and on that point, he disagreed.

I looked at my companion sitting next to me on the same plumped-up cushion for a seat. We had worked days and nights together for that last month, but as I looked at his face, I realized that regardless, despite all the time we had spent together debating the wording of a clause of a contract, ruminated over the warranties and indemnities and whether they would cover all the eventualities, in summary were we sure our client couldn't get screwed? But for all the time we had spent together, we really and truly didn't know each other at all. Not a bit.

He was a youngish Partner, and my mind went crazy with assumptions about him. I presumed he got his place at Princeton due to his parents. He never had to try before or after, to get ahead that is. From the precocious invites to the dinner party table as a child, from an early age, everyone bulked up his ego; "he was a star debater". He was both the center of attention and the kid on one of those television shows with a freaky talent that the parents have forced on their poor child. You know, tell us something, do a dance, sing a song, something posh, make us feel better?

"Where are you really from?" the colleague asked me through the noise and with a hint of a misplaced flirt.

"Are you Chinese?" He asked before I had to explain anything about Salinas. He couldn't tell from my name which part of Asia I was really from, even though we had worked together for months now.

He told me he loved Vietnamese movies, Apocalypse Now, Platoon, Full Metal Jacket…all the obvious ones…..he questioned whether it was traumatic for me to watch those movies, even if I hadn't seen them. Obviously, I had seen some of the movies he mentioned, and I thought of my dad's slob girlfriend watching them drinking Jack Daniels and raining chips all over her Harley

Davidson shirt. I didn't give him the satisfaction of an answer that would have most likely led to a racist comment. I just gave him the look I had perfected all these years. You know, the poker face.

In our project, all we had talked about was the work in front of us. I looked down the table at the rest of the engagement team drinking champagne and nibbling on canapes and realized I was pretty trapped next to this guy, and the only way to escape was to leave. Just get up and go. So, I exercised my right to do so.

As it turned out, the place was like a casino or a shopping mall, it was almost impossible to find a way out. There was more than one bar in this faux Asian den with a techno thump, and I found myself, after two wrong turns and a set of steps, in a more intimate cocktail bar. It still had an Asian theme. There was a red dragon mural on the wall and a long wall-to-wall marble bar. Most importantly, there was no techno and instead a really small jazz band in the corner, which competed with the buzz of chatter in the room. The circular red leather booths that lined the wall opposite the bar were filled with an altogether different crowd. In short, it appeared to be couples and not a corporate crowd. I paused and thought I would have one drink before going home for a much-needed sleep. So, I picked a random stool at the bar.

I recognized the song the band was playing, "Cheek to Cheek," by Ella Fitzgerald and Louis Armstrong, and I instantly felt my heart rate begin to slow a little.

I sat at the bar and took a breath of relief. I closed my eyes for a moment. A breath of freedom, if you will.

The bar was surrounded by bamboo and ornaments of pandas. The barman, or sorry mixologist, was soon in front of me looking for my order;

"What will it be?" He asked.

"A Cosmo, please?" I said, which instantly made me smile mischievously. I felt relieved to have escaped my colleagues. It was like I had been a submariner for the past few weeks, all cooped up with the other sailors, fixated on executing our plan, following orders, and eating rations with no place to go. You know, no escape.

The girl next to me was speaking to me, and she mouthed, "You look like the only person in this place who looks happy?"

I smiled my Mona Lisa smile. "Maybe," it said.

I turned to study the face of my newfound detective.

"Ha, don't be fooled. It's a sarcastic smile!" I was instantly disarmed.

"Ha," she added after taking a sip of her cocktail; "ok, a happy bitch then!"

Sandy Nicolson

The barman was saying something about making an exception, and it was no ordinary Cosmo blah blah blah.

Neither of us were listening to him, and instinctively, she reached over and touched my hand with a look that teased me. And that is how I met Lauren.

I was shaken from my walk down memory lane and noticed the muni was nearing my stop. The "retired" investment banker next to me seemed to be getting more conscious. He was staring at me; like in his presumably opioid state, he had somehow been listening to my thoughts the whole journey.

I found myself looking at him, and he sprung into life by abstractly saying to me abruptly, "Go on?" At the same time, I suddenly felt guilty at my indulgence and the fact that I sat next to this human being for nearly an hour but yet knew nothing about him but made all these assumptions. Shame on me, really.

We were pulling up 20th close to Mission Dolores Park, and it was indeed my stop.

I didn't answer him but instead rose from my seat. In due course, I shuffled out to the aisle. I chimed the cord to indicate for the driver to take the next stop and the bus obediently began to slow down. The failed investment banker continued to stare at me through my movements. I suddenly felt compelled to do one act of kindness

Bonsai

on my birthday. I paused before walking down the aisle. I turned back to my Muni companion and presented him with my father's birthday envelope. He held it in his hands for a moment like it was a gift from afar. He gave me a look that said, really, life is, well, crazy. The contents of the envelope he would find in due course; "best of luck," I said politely and gave him a "Lily" smile.

Soon enough, I was on the sidewalk, and the karma must have worked immediately, as it had stopped raining.

Sandy Nicolson

Chapter 5

Lauren's secret

In our two-year relationship, Lily and I had hardly ever fought. At least not about anything significant. Petty stuff is what we usually bugged over, for the most part. She had worked through the night and never came home from the office and didn't answer her phone; "I got lost in the brief," she would protest, when I challenged her. Or when I supposedly left a shambles of leftover Chinese boxes across the kitchen, leaving it looking like there had been a police bust of a gang just as they sat down to eat their supper after their heist. She was so particular about the apartment being perfectly tidy all the time. My slovenliness reminded her of someone she liked much less years ago. Or so, she would protest.

Or I never paid anything towards the checks (or even know what they were), apparently, that was a common bug bear.

Or on my side, she never had anything to talk about over dinner on a Saturday night, apart from her office and team. Those sorts of things, as I say, were all pretty meaningless arguments on the face of it. But of course, sometimes those little things can belie more important movements under the earth's crust. I get that. Like the dog that starts barking in Los Angeles when there is a movement in the San Andreas fault starting in Central California so many miles away, there is an earthquake coming, the animal is trying to tell us. Woof, woof. Sure dog.

If I am being picky, it was mostly Lily who had the sort of pet peeves that instigated the conversation moving South. My take, anyway, was that the undercurrent of most of the niggles was the big unsaid. "You come from privilege, a family where money (and importantly, wasting it) didn't have the same value. It was her own insecurity for the most part, but maybe there was some truth to it sometimes. I'll acknowledge that, maybe a sentinel. But then again, like many couples, it was also true that we didn't really know our respective experiences in our lives before we met. It was more complex than that. And so, this usually meant, at any given diner out, we went back to listening to Lily talk about work and her team.

There was one other topic that had been emerging recently that was causing a more serious swell in our relationship. That topic was titled; "Moving in together on a permanent basis". I flippantly batted the topic back with something along the lines of, "But we do really live together". For the most part, that was true, and we had done so for over a year in the one-bedroom apartment that she rented off of 20th on Dolores in the Mission area. An area, if you haven't been there, well, it has been bohemian forever. It was technically true that I did still own my apartment (which my father bought me for my graduation). That piece of real estate was completely different. It had once upon a time belonged in a New York Times Weekend Magazine spread titled; "The chicest apartment in San Francisco" or something like that. I hated it nearly as much as my father. It was ostentatious, a symbol of deep privilege, and so unwanted. So, most of the time, it floated in the sky like a surreal ghost ship filled with the produce of fancy furniture stores. It was situated in arguably the best apartment block in San Francisco. You know, the kind with an awning and a doorman standing like a guard out front, like the White House or similar.

It was one of those apartment blocks you might have seen in a movie or a classic advert with a San Francisco montage in the background. The man on the doors party trick was knowing your name and escorting you to an old elevator you have to pull the wrought iron gate to get into, which, of course, you didn't want to hurt his feelings after standing, otherwise, without purpose for the duration of the day. The residents had become used to the magnificent sweeping views of the bay from the Golden Gate Bridge to Alcatraz. "I suppose it is a great view," they would tell their guests coyly. It was for all those reasons that I hated it, but at the same time, you see, I needed to be there. Otherwise, I would never be able to conceal my other life. However bad that may sound to you as a confession of sorts, it was absolutely necessary. It was only through owning it I was able to conceal my profession as an undercover police officer. Of course, you might say I could simply have bought

Bonsai

a more modest apartment. In truth, I don't really have a compelling defense for that other than maybe a complete paradox. On the one hand, I was completely indifferent to searching real estate listings, which would be a pretty pathetic excuse. More authentically, I kept it, not just a safe place where I would keep items relevant to my profession (my gun, for example), but most importantly, it reminded me of the reasons I joined the force and despised unchecked avarice and basically, wealthy crooks, like my father. I know that is sort of twisted. I get it, really give me a break.

On the other hand, Lily's place was a cozy lair where we could curl up like two cats. Call me a hypocrite, but I adored the chintzy rustic, eclectic chic of the artisan Mission neighborhood. In contrast, it was the home of the folks I was a defender of, in my mind anyway. The deprived, the abused, the injured, the addicts, the hookers, the members of society that my father's people used and abused every day.

The geography of Lily's apartment was tiny. The queen-sized bed took up the entire bedroom. The kitchen and lounge room were all one. To use real estate speak of "open plan" would give you the wrong impression. Whereas my apartment had the untouched, unlived picture of an upmarket catalog still, Lily's place had all the interior chic of the eclectic zoo that was a Jimmy Hendrix outfit. A true ode to hipster chaos. One wall of the lounge was full of mirrors, and the other carpet. You felt like you were in some kind of Lewis Carrol creation. Am I the right way around? You might think as you lay on the bed. It was the converse to my daily life and that is why I loved it.

The landlord's old black and white pictures of San Francisco in the 1950s still hung on the walls of the bedroom, giving me the feeling that I was that detective in one of those cop shows set in the 1970s that made policing cool to me growing up. You could sit for hours with a coffee at the window and look out at the crazies acting out below for hours. You didn't need a television for drama. There was a new scene playing out, at least every 20 minutes, on the streets below. The music of blaxploitation movies hummed in the air alongside mothers shouting at their children, and the screech of tires of cars filled with folks intent on breaking the system. But like the wallpaper in Lily's tiny bathroom that had begun to peel, there was change afoot, and the area was slowly being gentrified.

When Lily would say, well if you like this place so much, why don't we buy it and renovate? It made me cringe. As Bob Dylan once said, times were changing, and with it, my romantic view of the 70s and what these streets had been up until now inspired my chosen profession. Well, they would never be the same again.

Lily's cause for a joint real estate commitment had nothing to do with her wanting to stay in my swanky apartment, which, as I

Bonsai

say, you know, my dad gave me. It was more a desire to show that this apartment that she had taken as a staffer in her law firm was not appropriate for her new standing as a Partner. The years she had worked in the Office, barely having time to sleep in this place represented why she now hated it, quite the opposite from my feeling. The squalor of the neighborhood disgusted her every day as she walked to and from the Muni. Our politics, which we rarely discussed, was so crazy far apart. While I was (unbeknownst to her) the superhero champion to these people, the locals if you will, fighting the good fight to save our liberal society, she was, honestly, and maybe I am exaggerating, but she was right of Ghengis Khan.

"Do these people have no self-respect? She had been born with nothing like them, but unlike them, she had dignity. She would protest. With just her brains and hard work and determination, she had fought her way to the top, well, in her world at least. It could be done, and she knew how she would announce proudly. What's wrong with policing? She would say with menace and somewhat teasingly, but of course, I wouldn't say, "I am chasing the real bad guys, the corporate crooks that are exploiting these people, from the very peak of the layer cake. So far, at the top of white privilege, they think they are untouchable. Take out those folks, and everyone else will rise!" I would say in my head triumphantly. Shucks, I couldn't tell her that.

Sandy Nicolson

It may seem perverse, but with one major exception, I actually enjoyed that our politics were different. Sort of the opposites attract, really, in more ways than one. And somewhat macabre when she bought me toy handcuffs to use for one Valentines, I will be honest, it was a turn-on, piqued by the secret and dangerous truth about my real profession. In some ways, whilst I wasn't as intellectually gifted as her, my secret gave me power perversely, it gave me a sense of possession of a dangerous truth. I spent my life committing to locking up the bad guys, but in the bedroom, I would submit to her. I knew something important that she didn't. And you know that perversion gave me a thrill.

The one aspect of this discordant argument, in complete contrast to our opposite politics, that made me cringe was the other reason that she wanted us to buy an upgraded apartment together is so she could have a proper place to entertain her team as a Partner. In equal measure, I detested the proposition as it was so insincere, as was evident every Saturday over dinner together. She hated her team. Each team member, one with gusto. Absolutely and completely she did and I am not going to bore you with it.

So what was the real purpose of this "entertaining" proposition? Was it it to impress on them that she was better than them somehow. It didn't make sense to me and, of course, it represented a world I had fled from, and conversely, she flew to it

Bonsai

like a fly in a restaurant or gas station store, flew to an insect buzzer foolishly attracted by the light. All that that world represented appalled me; the society parties, little trays of hors d'oeuvres appetizers, meaningless manners, and pretentious discussions that floated in the air like poison. Yuk.

Of course, there could also have been an argument that she just wanted me to commit to her in a way that provided needed evidence that I sincerely loved her, and she was just inelegant about making that point, but I wasn't ready to consider that yet and especially because of my own parents disastrous marriage, which made it impossible for me to commit to material ties, like a real estate partnership, representing a marriage of sorts, at least not yet. Do you get that about me? Anyway, I don't care if you do or don't.

There was maybe one other aspect of our relationship that was increasingly becoming more significant and maybe a byproduct of this commitment discussion, which was my occasional distrust of Lily's long hours. It was pathetic in a way because if it weren't for the fact she was such a workaholic, I wouldn't have been able to disguise my own long, and unconventional hours as a cop. It was undoubtedly wrapped up in the fact that she was the first serious lover in my life (or, more precisely, one that lasted more than a one-night stand or, say, a couple of months). She was certainly the only one I had "lived" with. Anyway, don't tell her, but you get the irony of that last statement.

I am sharing a lot with you here, but I can actually be more genuine than that. More authentic, sure, here goes. I was insecure about how gay she really was. I actively looked for signs of it. When we made love, obviously, but also when we were out with friends or talking about trivial entertainment stuff. You know. How sincere was she? Was she, in any sense of it, faking it? Could that be a reflection of my own lies too about those other aspects of our relationship manifesting, I am no psychologist, but it is possible, of course.

But most of all, given how ruthless she was about getting to the top and making it to the Partnership, at her firm, which clearly represented so much to her. The question that killed me? Ate me up on a bad day without question? Would she sleep with a guy at work? A more senior colleague, a client, one of those types, particularly appalled me. How could I handle that? It would have been much more of a dagger to my heart than just some drunk guy at a bar hitting on her.

On my worst nights, I am not proud of this, and please don't judge me. I don't know if you would, but you know it would usually be triggered by some vice bust experience, men doing despicable things, Men doing things to young girls or sleazy men at the top of some criminal endeavor, that if I would follow through a stakeout

Bonsai

which revealed that they were cheating on their wives, anyway, crappy things I witnessed. On those nights, you know, I would stake out my own girlfriend. How sick is that? I would sit in my Ford Wagon, watching her lone office light on the sixth floor late at night with the solitary light on.

I was watching for a shadow of a man to appear and prove me right.

Or I would slip into a restaurant where a late-night client dinner was happening and watch in disguise for the hint of a flirt from one of her clients at the table. Yes, I tortured myself like that.

Please don't judge me for these thoughts. I share them in confidence. Of course, I am not sure if all relationships decay, with these types of paper cuts that build into a million bleeds over time. It's a subject that has obviously haunted me since my childhood. I'll acknowledge that, for what it's worth. Am I self-sabotaging our relationship, me and Lily here? I ask myself. Maybe.

To think, when I met Lily in a cocktail bar in Palo Alto, it was all so perfect, so innocent in some ways, but maybe not really. Maybe, I read it wrong. We shared a look, and I just fell in love at first sight. As our conversation subsequently unfolded, she asked me simply.

"Why are you here? I mean, in this bar tonight? Why?"

She then said something that a guy would for sure have messed up, "Are you an angel from heaven;" or similar banal shit to get in my pants. Instead, she added sincerely, "Are you here to help me escape?" It was meaningful, well I fell in love with her, for goodness sake.

We made love that first night and found ourselves in a coffee shop in the financial district on Stockton and Battery, near her office, the next day. From those first meetings, at that point, we didn't want to be apart. In those days, wow, not for a minute did we want to be separate. How did that change?

At one point in the coffee shop, she asked.

"No, really, why are you here?" It was disarming, as I could see the sharpness in her forensic lawyer's eyes continually feeding her brain with its voracious appetite for detail. Tell me why? They said, equally, there was a disarming innocence to her tone, like she had already fallen for me.

"I'm so grateful you are suddenly here," is what I heard in my head.

I figured the owner could just afford the high rent of the space and, so, the spartan design was deliberate, e.g. stripped back and meant to be cool, I suppose. The patrons were meant to fill the canvas as folks walked by outside and created the picture on both sides of the glass that faced the street. For some reason, it created a recall of my mother's interior design magazines she was so obsessed with as she constantly remodeled our Atherton family mansion through the years growing up. If it was a design intent, then the interior was deliberate post-modern (an ode to Phillippe Starck or those guys that are into bleak, minimalist stuff, I was convinced of it. For some reason, the memory of my mother triggered my lie. I am quite impressed with myself. I remember that designer, I think that's his name, who knows.

"I am an interior designer, and I designed this place," I told Lily, adding as if to make my selection of a coffee house romantic; "that is why I suggested it!" The truth, of course, was that it had caught my attention on a late-night drive back to our station on Battery and California one night recently, as a 24-hour coffee house that was near the station. To add extra romance, I doubled down on the lie further;" and said, " That is why I suggested, here, you know, I wanted you to see my work".

"Wow! Amazing! My god, your talented babe".

It turned out, from a practical perspective, to be a perfect lie. Try Googling who designed a coffee shop interior near you. Pretty impossible to find, never mind verify. And with the morning rush hour traffic in San Francisco Financial District, it was obviously extremely unlikely she was going to ask the barista (who, at any rate, would expect a latte or chai tea order and look at you blankly otherwise). "Sorry, we don't have that here;" would likely be the answer even if you did get a response of sorts to. "Who designed the place?" Sure. Another crazy person. Next customer, please.

For some reason, I justified all this, at first, with the fact that telling most people you're a cop on the first date, well, it creates a level of suspicion that, right or wrong, I thought was too risky, to tell the truth! I would tell her at the right point, I would say to myself. It just has never happened, and I have since gone too deep now, well, deep cover, if you will. There was no way back now.

Also, I don't know if it was her unconscious bias, my blonde hair, blue eyes, and Palo Alto background that made that answer so perfect for her. Stereotypically, I fitted the bill. Of course, that made perfect sense, a commercial interior designer? I immediately stepped into the character she wanted to sleep with and have simply never left that role. I am good at this type of thing, being undercover, assuming other identities, and lying, I suppose. Lily wasn't a crook, of course. She was my girlfriend, a lawyer, literally blossoming with integrity. But my lie was a big lie, and like any big lie, once I had committed to it. It was impossible to go back.

So, she accepted the authenticity of my answer without question and launched into teasing me about design, as if I really was the designer. So when I told her I designed the bar we met in and was modestly offended at her lack of appreciation for my Asian notes, well, she chided me flirtatiously.

"It wasn't a complete disaster!" she said.

"So, you're the one to blame for the faux Asian cushions and that whole contemporary vogue Asian thing at that place. That's the type of thing in vogue these days? Really? Maybe I can help you with that now?" she teased, and I went with it.

"Like I said. I could tell you were a bitch;" and I smiled indulgently.

She apologized for being such a bitch, and we laughed. But in truth, I was the bitch for not telling her the truth. You see, the truth was, I was a forensic cop, of course, and more specifically, I had been undercover at the time. And in some ways, I had been using Lily from the first time we met on that day. She helped cover my cover, and this might seem strange, but I actually fell in love with her because of that.

Chapter 6
How Bonsai Met His Friend

Montgomery and I would often play rounds of golf without really talking to each other in the early days. He called me Bonsai, sure, and I called him Montgomery, sometimes Monty to begin with. Not until I knew him better did I call him "Captain".

In other words, we would address each other by name, but following that, we wouldn't say anything really that otherwise resembled more than perfunctory comments. The kind of economic dialogue that folks exchange on a golf course any given day of the week. These are really monosyllabic, skinny-down conversations that especially folks of my vintage feel most comfortable with. Phrases like;

After you?

Nice shot!

You're playing well today.

That's the game, huh?

Fore right!!

I didn't see where you went.

Your honor!

Bonsai

In other words, the polite, civil language of golf. It may tell you a little about the civility of a person, their manners, their interest in how you're playing, how you feel would be too far, but how you're playing? Sure.

I suppose if you were really stalking a fellow player, or more commonly, you were critiquing the Pro on television, then sure, you might combine those little details with a broader picture. What I mean is a deeper perspective on a person, you know, beyond their golf game per se. So, if you watch a game, you'll see a commentator say something like;

"Of course (insert player) has had a tough personal time recently, etc." or "he is fulfilling his promise now. Nice shot".

In that type of instance, you are able to be like an amateur detective and build a narrative more broadly than simply their golf game. That is what brings brilliance to sport and that game when you listen to a really good golf commentator or sports commentator for that matter. They have to be great storytellers. Otherwise, well, it's boring to watch a sport when you're not playing, for most folks anyways. But those folks can bring the sport it to life with their narratives, even for someone who doesn't play the game.

"Shucks, I didn't know his wife had cancer. Wow, and he is leading the tournament in spite of that. Wow," they might say. And so you lean in. Will the player fall apart or be inspired by the adversity?

Sandy Nicolson

But that type of exchange is for the commentators. On the course, I am not saying we resort to cave people, but as I say, the everyday golf chat is much more military, skinied down than that. There is a code, a brevity to exchanges that happens in the day to day rounds. There are unspoken rules on what can and can't be covered in the conversation between players.

We were older men who wanted the opposite from a deep, intense exchange on, say, political subjects of the day, or our health (especially our health), or a controversy of the day. Golly, those are the last things we wanted to exchange notes on. Instead, we wanted a narrative as narrow as a look at say a putt. No extra color was needed. In that way, the only thing we wanted to read was the greens, not each other. You could say we were a couple of old curmudgeons that way. But that would be your misread, and our conversations developed over time to reveal a different arc. A different understanding of each other.

In the beginning, we had absolutely no interest in the details, large or small, about the other's life, no sir, to be shared with spoken word at any rate, in those early years. It was an unspoken thing that isn't uncommon among men our age who play golf. No, we didn't seek that out. Rather, we played to escape all of that detail of life to some extent, of course. Our rounds in this way were to us sort of a version of heaven we felt we may deserve, in our golden years, on a good day at any rate. In other words, even if, on any given day, our game, our respective moods, or even the weather was not up to scratch, at least the game and experience of play gave us some teasing premise of some form or prospect of peace. That is why we would come back again and again, searching for it, that serenity. Just to be clear, even with the passing of each round, that premise wasn't fully lived out. The mere familiarity of our economic language and functional behavior, e.g. your shot, my shot, even if that were just it, even the nods and the grunts, the hand gestures, that alone gave us some form of solace approaching closure to our lives. As I say, it is something approaching peace of mind and spirit. I may not do that thought complete justice, but I hope you get the point.

The language etiquette, the rule book of the game we followed meticulously, was black and white, simple and clear, even if everything else in life was ultimately unpredictable. In that way, if you were to read this situation well, that played out for us every couple of weeks, if you joined our group one day, say, with an aspiration for a deeper conversation with two strangers, and thought about it afterward, about the lack of color in our discussion, if you were really insightful, you would realize these were two old men, bound together like ancient tribesman that didn't need to say it, they both knew they did this because they wanted to escape the complexities of life they had respectively. They had given up trying to understand and had found a place (the golf course) where they could simply accept and be accepted in some way in each other's company.

In that way, the golf course had become the metaphor for those things. We knew we would never shoot the perfect round as many times as we played, that answer would forever elude us. It was out of reach now. But you know that was okay. And that acceptance made us wise men for those four hours, or so it took to play a round. In fact, the more we played together, the more we noticeably aged, the more our bodies gave way to the ground and time, and the more, in a funny way, that was maybe the only thing that ultimately made some sense. Sure, we are getting older. Got it!

We both knew that we had a past. Of course, we did. We had lived to a certain age. That much was plain as day. But that transactional relationship, if you like, I am describing that was in the early rounds before we got to know each other more sincerely. Our relationship began to change with each round that we played together as friends.

Vignettes of our past inevitably began to slip out as time passed, into our discussion. I won't bore you with the inconsequential stuff but let me give you a quick picture of how it worked. Someone would say, "Great shot, hey, I won't bore you with this, but you know...

We became less contrite and less controlled as we became

Bonsai

more comfortable with each other. The more intently we tried to keep this monk-like existence on the course, the more we failed. Things would begin to leak out like a political news story, piece by piece. You know, "Breaking news!" In very small increments, little morsels of our lives, we would share with each other, and, you know, as a consequence, we became closer to each other as a result.

"I didn't know you had a daughter?"

"You used to live on the East Coast?"

"You played high school football? I didn't know that".

Banal details and uncomplicated stuff to begin with. But in the end, we couldn't hold back in sharing the more significant stuff. He became a great friend, and likewise, it was, I don't know destiny if you will, we wanted to tell each other, you know, our stories, who and what we loved, and why.

Perhaps it's the doubt of what comes next that makes any other person share their life story as they approach the inevitability of death. Little by little, you are confessing to someone who becomes a close friend, whether you like it or not. The desire to find someone who is empathetic to your journey, even given your fear that you might not find understanding from them. You seek comfort that you ultimately did your best, did the right thing, and even if you didn't, you shouldn't regret it. We all make mistakes you want to hear from someone else. Regardless of the fear, something compels you to share your truth, and that is precisely what happened between my friend Monty and me as we got to know each other through our rounds of golf.

On paper, Monty was ostensibly closer to whatever day of reckoning than I was in years anyway. And as much as I kept my eyes on the road or fairway, so to speak, in those early years, his leg and back troubles became harbingers of a change in the form of our conversations as we would begin to creak around the course, as our age crept forward and well, the inevitably of life snuck up on us.

It wasn't until Monty began to miss games and began to apologize that "the glacier slowly melted," and I saw my friend in more color. At first, in minimalist terms, he would only say, "I am slowing you down today". "No, sir, don't worry about it," I would reply, but not being too deep about it. Of course, he was one of my best friends, you know, I noticed it, the aging.

But golf is ultimately a game of etiquette, and I think as he began to become more aware of his own inability to keep up with play, he felt obliged to share a bit more about himself.

"This is the right thing to do," you could hear him think.

And so little by little droplets of paint would trickle onto the canvas if you like, and well you know, created the picture of his life

Bonsai

just for me.

We never spoke about our race or ethnicity. He was black, and I was Asian American, of course. His story had important roots in his race, though. I felt that when he told me, and honestly, no offense, I simply won't do it justice.

Golf isn't a game known as a vehicle for the pioneering of equality and rights historically. So depending on the course we played, believe it or not, even in the 21st century, we could see the prejudices in others that were still there. We saw it in technicolor or whatever the latest and most clear and lucid version there may be of that. And we would look at each other. Nothing needed to be said. Things that we would experience would be similar to the following;

I'm sorry we don't have a tee available for you folks (when the tee box was wide open).

Seriously?

Excuse me, do you folks work here?

What country are you from?

Or the avoidance of a handshake and the end of a round.

Or, in the 19th hole, comments like, "This area is taken". Sure.

Unfortunately, racism or unconscious bias still existed, but of course, not between me and my friend.

Whenever we experienced these things, in most of the cases, we had no other power than to cover our ears. After all, the pursuit of peace and the avoidance of conflict was what we sought from playing the game. On the flip side, each time that we played and didn't experience it, each time we were shown respect, each time someone sincerely spoke about Tiger's achievements, we did draw some kind of solace from that, we did find some kind of belief, howsoever incrementally, that there was change happening for the better, albeit too slow.

So, when Monty started to share his stories with me, his truth, in this context, was truly remarkable to me. Whilst I was a self-employed immigrant who had a daughter who went to Stanford, for which, despite my personal flaws, I was incredibly proud to have lived up to American values in spite of challenges. In Monty's case, when I reflected at that point in our relationship on the many racist encounters we had over the years on the course, the stoicism, self-restraint, and grace that he had shown in spite of it all, in retrospect, suddenly burned my eyes with pride.

You see, when he shared with me the cause of his injuries being the result of his service years ago for the country, I had an altogether profound respect for my dear friend.

You see, he was one of the first African Americans to make

Bonsai

the rank of Captain in the Army of his generation. I think that is the rank he said, I've never used the internet, and I am not a library guy, but I never doubted him. Please do look it up. I am pretty sure it's true.

I had got to know him all these years ago, and it all made sense now that he was an army man. I knew that to reach the rank of Officer at any level for a man of his generation was an incredible accomplishment.

I was incredibly proud that he was my friend, in a much deeper way, after that simple disclosure.

It was ironic, of course, given my heritage, that his first tour had been in the Korean War and many tours in Vietnam thereafter before retiring to Monterey (where he had trained at one point and originally met his wife). When he retired, he followed his wife's wishes and returned to where they had raised their children. In time, he would tell me he became a history teacher, and when his wife died of breast cancer in her 60s, he retired to the golf course and played with mostly strangers, mostly tourists or tech workers visiting from San Francisco and then, of course, myself. He mostly played with people who wouldn't ask personal questions.

So, one of the additional bonds we had that developed as our friendship deepened was that we were men without women and that our children had flown to not return. Albeit, what led us to meet each other were two very different paths.

When we broke into those discussions (and without me saying, as his leg made it harder and harder for him to play golf), these conversations, when we actually began to talk, changed venue from the golf course to the room at the rear in my garage. If we had been like some married couples the arc of our relationship was inverted. The rich conversations were not at the start but much later on.

My moment to share more of my story happened one evening very late in the fall when the last remaining leaves clung to their branches in the hopes that summer wouldn't end. It was not long after we both began sharing more than functional golf exchanges with each other (and making like much younger men in return).

It was soon after Monty shared all this with me that it became my turn to share the equivalent of his life story about the shrapnel he caught in his leg when he bailed from a "Huey" chopper under fire near the border of Thailand in 1971 that caused him such pain these days on the course and sent him to Monterey to teach. In my case, the "shrapnel" was there in my heart, but it wasn't physical. Well, we will get to that real soon. Don't worry, I just need to build up to it.

Chapter 7
Bonsai Tells Monty His Truth

Indeed, it was more mental hurt rather than physical shrapnel that was the corollary of the life story that I would share with Monty. Something that had hurt me deeply and left a piece of proverbial shrapnel deep under the skin beyond the naked eye and, after its insertion. It has hampered my ability to form normal human relationships ever since. Anyway, there you go, for what it's worth.

So, just to be clear, now that Monty and I were beginning to talk more and enjoy exchanges beyond perfunctory golf vocabulary, that doesn't mean we had replaced that with a singsong. No, our exchanges were still staccato and succinct in form. It was just that the content had expanded beyond golf. The door was proverbially ajar but still only slightly.

It actually happened only last week when we had just finished a round, and we headed in our customary fashion to the carpark to say our farewells and arrange the time of our next game. Monty, in a somewhat stubborn fashion, had objected to having an electric cart that day despite his leg bothering him (so it was probably the slowest round we had ever played). So, he shuffled, and I followed him to his car, you know, after the round. His car was modest, as you might expect of the man I've described to you so far, a 93" Toyota Camry (that would become the best serviced Camry in California, and maybe, just maybe, in the United States in due course). If it is not obvious, I loved Monty. He was and is a dear friend.

As I loaded my bag in my truck parked side by side with him, I could see he was struggling to get it started. The car that is.

I got out of my truck and knocked on the window. The window wound down in the old-fashioned way and at his own pace. Nothing was hurried. Swizzle, swizzle. Sure, I am waiting. Not like these days, when everything is instantaneous, you know, on demand!

He was probably thinking I was about to change our tee time plan for our next match. Instead, I simply said, "All of these years, you've maybe noticed, but there is always a little oil on my hands".

"Oil?"

He looked at me, puzzled as if to say why would get it into the way of his obvious angst to encourage his car to start with such a seemingly abstract comment. I explained that I was a mechanic.

"Oh, sure, makes sense, erm what's your point?"

I raised an eyebrow in return.

It didn't take long for me to get some life back into the old

Bonsai

Camry. I may have been mediocre at golf, but I was a hell of a mechanic and I told him so, and well, I am pretty proud to tell you.

I convinced Monty that we could drive back to my garage, and I would fix the car properly for him. Leaving my truck in the public car park of Pacific Grove, a relatively sleepy town, wasn't going to be a problem, and anyway, the "fog would hide it anyway," I added, referring to the clouds sweeping in from the Pacific. I honestly don't know why I added that poetry.

He acquiesced, and soon, I was driving his injured Camry back to my garage.

When we got there, the sun had gone from the big Salinas Valley sky and was replaced with a sky that looked like a black sequined dress worn at a 1920s speakeasy.

I owned the only truly independent Gas station left in Salinas, a true relic. I mean, a true dinosaur! Maybe one of the only ones in the Salinas Valley, who knows. It was a building that, if you drove down from San Francisco and were, an artist, the sight of it in the midday sun surrounded dramatically by fields as far as the eye could see filled with artichokes and strawberry crops would make you want to take a picture of it.

The picture would likely be good enough that it could even end up being sold in a market stall to tourists on Embarcadero in a

Sandy Nicolson

basket alongside pictures of the Golden Gate Bridge, Alcatraz, The Painted Ladies, Yosemite, etc. and then sentimentally you would turn over the 6 by 4 prints to one of my old Salinas Garage, a true relic of a bygone time.

The old gas station pumps would remind some sentimentally of the times when people like me would fill up your car, like a Cadillac Coupe DeVille or old Chevy in a boiler suit and flat cap and you would be sitting waiting to maybe hand me a tip. An old classic Esso sign hung from the canopy of the forecourt, which I had never gotten around to taking down even though it flapped in the wind and made a god-awful noise. It sang "hee haw;" like a donkey every other day.

At high noon, when the structure was fully lit up, you could see just how much in disrepair it was. Like an old actor without their makeup on you could notice it wasn't the same as it once was.

The paint of the outbuildings was flaking, like the cracked chocolate topping on a child's ice cream. I am not a great writer, so, you know, I can't do this justice, but the building was elegance fading if you get the picture.

Yes, my block of concrete was a dying memory of another time. Another time was when Monty and I were young, and the so-called gas-guzzling automobiles ruled America.

Bonsai

The tourist I'm talking to you about at the market in San Francisco, you know, the one that might have bought the picture. If they hung it in their kitchen, and looked at it, much later, more closely one day with their morning coffee, they may eventually notice the sad Asian man in the store, looking out, they would stand back from their kitchen table to study him more closely. And with that squint at the picture, it may suddenly change in form, take a different shape, and the romance would give way to hope lost, a sense of something tragic and maybe haunting would take over.

"I think I have missed something, you know, I am not sure what," the tourist would say to whoever would listen, say their wife.

The man looks sad, you would likely conclude, though, the guy in the gas station, no doubt about that.

I think we will take this picture down, they might say (a year or two later after their trip), I remembered it otherwise as a good vacation. they would likely tell their partner, "Sorry, this picture gives me the spooks now for some reason….. No idea, but that guy, I didn't notice him until now, but you know, the way he is looking, out of the gas station, never mind, but don't you think it's a bit strange, you know, the way he gazes?

Notwithstanding my presence in the picture, it would be right to interpret a tragedy in more ways than one. In the arc of history, the geo-political chaos, oil-based wars, and pending environmental disasters, my gas station had seen it all and was metaphorically tired. As I said, if you looked closer, the romance was surely gone in more ways than one. In fact, it was inevitable that, in time, this station would be abandoned and slowly rot into the ground and be at one with the origin of the fossil fuels that had once given its purpose. It was a true fossil of a place, who knows, maybe like me.

So, I was glad that when Monty and I pulled the Camry into the Station, the sky was dark and on a more superficial level, you know, it was a less embarrassing introduction to my friend of what I called an office.

Monty, after all, had spent a lifetime in his career polishing his shoes to look like mirrors and ensuring his dress uniform was constantly immaculate, so I didn't want the embarrassment of seeing the full disgrace of my place, that you know, I called home.

After we parked and I opened the gate to the work room, the Captain asked me, "Why don't you keep the garage open when you're not here, get some help when you're playing golf for example? You don't make money, otherwise. Anyway, I am just asking. Sorry, to pry".

I opened the door to my workshop, and the garage roller door opened with a whirl that I have heard a million times, but somehow noticed the whirl more that night. The garage seemed to have more

Bonsai

presence than usual. I turned on the light to illuminate the room. Maybe I was just being self-conscious, but it felt like the room that was my refuge for so many years from the store, from people, from questions, from life, you know, a rest post from work, where I worked on cars, worked on my trees or you know, and no shame in it, a place where I would just sit in my old seat and reminisce about what could have been or what might be.

I answered Monty's question, partly hoping I would distract him in the process from the squalor of my life that the bright light of the room was illuminating.

"Please, Monty, take a seat, and I'll tell you why. I hope you'll at least have a small drink with me now you have been to my cave. Please have a drink, and then I'll order a taxi for you. You'll be home in no time, really. I'll have your Camry ready in the morning for you. What do you say?".

Monty looked slightly awkward at the unexpected invitation, and then he nodded. Something about his gesture and the scene made me think of a different time for some funny reason when he would be carrying out his duty of visiting the home of the loved one of a member of his command who was never coming home. Obviously, this wasn't the same (not by a long stretch), but his movement, his gait if you like, made me think of that. Maybe it was just that he was being polite by saying yes and really wanted to get home. It could have been as basic as that, but there was something to his air, and maybe the rarity of having someone there with me made me think that way. Forgive me for being self-indulgent.

"Perfect," I said and ushered him to my only other seat that had been my Uncle's. I then added apologetically, I only have a scotch. I hope that's okay?

He simply nodded, that would do. For this type of moment, he had learned to exercise self-control. He held two fingers like he was indicating a crocodile, but in this case meant no more than "2 inches" poured, please.

I washed a glass and a coffee cup, the only two drinking vessels I had. It had been a long time since I had a visitor here. If you drove past the garage right at that point and looked in and saw these two ghostly figures in the decaying garage, you would naturally have sped up. "Geez, that place looks scary," you would likely blurt out. The ghostly two old men, sitting in a garage set amongst the darkened fields lit by the moon, would have been quite a sight, I bet.

"It's Laphroaig," I said, passing him the glass and precisely pouring "two fingers" and adding with a smile he barely returned, a rare sardonic joke; in reference to the drink, "it's like the courses round here, complex".

Bonsai

He gave a look back, that said, all I know is I accepted two inches of liquor.

I took it as an impatient signal to answer his question as we entered the room, so I immediately got into my seat and followed the order.

"Times have changed significantly since I moved here in 1970 or so. You see, to cut to the chase, my competition now, if you can even call it that, are the big box franchise chains; gas chains, the 76ers, the Chevron's, the Shell's around town, you know the types. You will have noticed as we drove here, to Old Stage Road, there are none of those around here. Nothing but fields and an inconvenient arterial road that only has a few through roads".

"That wasn't always the case. The roads connecting Salinas with other planets of civilization have changed all the way back to the Mexican occupiers really. The equivalent of Highway 101, between San Francisco and Salinas, Monterey, etc., was once upon a time right here, but bit by bit, all that changed with new roads, and slowly but surely, somehow, this road got orphaned and with it my gas station. An arterial road that got blocked, so to speak, from the heartland, and there has never been a bypass operation, so to speak".

"On top of that, all those fancy chains, of course, they have the money that I have never had to hop up sticks and move to a better spot, just like that. So staying open this time, in the hopes that somebody is lost, would be a waste of time. Slowly, but now at a much faster pace, I'm literally and physically running out of gas here. I have my old-time farmers that have come here partly due to loyalty to my Uncle, and partly due to my mechanical skills, but I simply can't compete with the gas prices whatsoever anymore. I make virtually nothing from that, and there is no loyalty anymore in those big farms or they have alliances nationally with the chains. As for being a mechanic, well, these new generations of cars and trucks, shucks. Well, your Camry is a treat for me, 1993, I can do that, but these new vehicles, even if I had kept up with new-fangled technology, I couldn't afford the equipment to fix them".

I nearly told him then that the only reason we hadn't died out long ago was also because I was a damn good poker player, one of the best and won in all kinds of games up and down the Peninsula until I ran out of capital and luck, of course.

However good you are at poker, it's a hopeless game if you don't have the funds. Eventually, no matter how much you might go on a lucky run, sooner or later, you will lose if your opponent has more capital.

Of course, I had become addicted to the game, and that's why I had desperately borrowed foolishly from the street and now was deeply in debt. I still had some pride left and a disused condom machine with my last ten thousand dollars that may win me out of

Bonsai

the hole yet. Maybe, if I was lucky.

With my pause, his gaze fell to his left, and my little study station, my gallery, and, of course, my forest of clippings documenting Lily's achievements from elementary school to the present day. At least the ones I knew about.

He took a sip of the Laphroaig. In the failing light of my garage, I felt like the scotch was playing tricks on me. My friend was no longer the old man I knew but the Officer he once was. A leader who was used to the awful task of conversing with the bereaved or anyone like me who has lost something precious and without saying it, you likely just knew I had a sad set of circumstances. Maybe he knew that from the very start. He could read it in my face.

He didn't skip a beat and was on his feet. Momentarily, the bad leg was gone, instead, a much younger Monty, an officer, had stood with precision from his chair and was by the picture and soon caught the pinned excerpt from the San Francisco chronicle. It looked, to me at least, that he was giving my homage to Lily the respect of a war memorial.

"Youngest in her class," the Captain noted.

"You must be very proud indeed:" he added with some gravitas.

Sandy Nicolson

In the days when our exchanges were not as profound, I had told him that I had a daughter who lived in San Francisco but no more than that. Now, he had the fuller picture due to my tribute to her on the wall.

His authoritative officer stare commanded my respect, and I proudly answered.

"Yes, Stanford scholarship and youngest Partner at the law firm she works at". I said and instantly thought a little too robotically.

To fill the silence, I put on some music, a favorite track of mine from a long time ago, struck up quietly in the background, like a fire coming to life to warm the room.

It opened with the line that had tortured me so many times.

The main chorus was something like this;

An old lover who burnt so bright

Only to disappear

Who knows?

But from my sight

All that I do know is I love you

Until and beyond loved one of old

Bonsai

I know you're out there somewhere

Old love of mine

The Captain caught me from my reverie with a purposive stare and said with an uncharacteristic, softer, concerned tone I hadn't heard before. It had a sincerity and genuine concern that was clear. He asked me very succinctly the question no one had ever cared to ask me directly, apart from Lily, for a very long time;

"What of her mother? If you don't mind me asking."

There was no dramatic crash of waves against rocks or howls of wind accompanied by the sirens of wildlife that had accompanied him, sharing the history of his army career with me on the golf course. In fact, quite the opposite, apart from a quiet murmur of that ancient song, there was no other soundtrack to our discussion.

In fact, there might as well have been silence in the room.

He was back in his seat with his whiskey glass, barely touched, and nodded to me as if to say. "Please go on. We are now friends, and this feels important. It feels like there is more to this". I knew that I didn't need to ask him if he had more time. But for me, the time had come to tell my truth.

So, I cleared my throat and slowly prepared myself to tell him why I could never leave this fossil park in the field somewhere in the Salinas Valley until it slowly started to sink into the ground with me inside it.

Monty was still staring at me. Waiting patiently for me.

I cleared my throat.

"Well, Captain, this is no ordinary story," I said almost apologetically for what had been my life.

"None of us are ordinary."

I nodded in agreement and looked at my Bonsai tree collection with a smile and suddenly saw it for its sudden peculiar inclusion to the stage we found ourselves in. How true, I thought.

"Well, I'll start this story somewhere familiar for you. Have you ever looked at those sheds you can see if you stand on the 12th tee at Del Monte Golf Club and look back to the Pacific? Those commercial warehouses? Commercially, they call them "sheds".

"Yes, I know them, full of rich people's treasures hidden from the public and the IRS too, most likely".

I smiled. "Well, one of those is where a very powerful man houses many of his most precious belongings. Some of the most beautiful works of art, pictures, vases, antiquities, classic cars. Millions of dollars of items all concealed from the world in one of those concrete boxes. You see, that is what this man does. He acquires beautiful things and keeps them from the light. Absolute possession is what he demands".

"Why does that interest you?" Monty said pointedly.

"Well, he possesses the most precious thing I have ever set my own eyes on".

"A picture?"

"No, the love of my life, Lily's mother".

"You mean he kidnapped her and ran off with her?"

"Not exactly, but he does own her".

"In what way?"

I saw his look of concern and answered, "No, not like a prostitute in the traditional sense, but she was something like that once upon a time."

"My friend, you know I am a simple man, and I truly want to understand your history here, but I am afraid you are talking in riddles presently".

The Captain suddenly looked uncomfortable.

"I understand that Captain. Like I said, this is a complicated story. It may be best if I start at the beginning of the story and bring you to the present day. Let me tell you how this fits together. How do you say it logically? Even though, in the end, it may defy logic, and I hope that doesn't unsettle you".

"I have seen many things in my life. Don't worry about surprising me about the human condition. Maybe tell me more about this powerful man and who he is precisely? ".

"Well, his name is Takeshi-san, a Japanese entrepreneur. He is one of the preeminent businessmen of the 21st century but like many men like that, he is a very dangerous man. I worked for him once as his driver when he visited his house in Pebble Beach. He returned to Japan and had to spend time in jail for some kind of irregularities. And I was entrusted to look after his beautiful wife in his absence. You know, drive her around and so forth.

"Lily's mother? Let me guess, the "so forth" became more than "so forth"?" he said without judgment.

I nodded and added by explanation, "She had seen what Takeshi could do. She knew what he would do if he ever found out."

The song lyric pulsed, *"only to disappear"*.

"She was convinced he would kill me and maybe even Lily. And so we could never be together, and the baby had to be hidden. Like in a fable from a long time ago. But for me, it was a hellish reality".

Bonsai

The Captain struggled to take in my disclosure. I wasn't sure what part of the story was more incredulous to him, but I landed on it being that Lily had to spend her childhood in this dark cave near Salinas, never knowing who her mother was.

"But you see, Captain, that is not the most incredible part. Yesterday, I had a visitor. A man who arrived in a much newer Toyota. As usual, it was a slow afternoon. I was about to close up for an afternoon siesta and listen to some jazz when I saw a car pull in, a plume of dust and a crunch of stones announcing its entrance. It was a brand new black Toyota Corolla. It pulled into the forecourt. I knew instantly it was a hired car. You get to spot these types of things when you own a garage like mine over the years.

It caught my interest immediately when a tall Japanese man, maybe in his early forties, got out of the car. Instantly, I could see there was something unusual about him. He had some kind of purpose. It was his poise. You see, there was a precision to his movements. A thought of a martial artist floated through my head, and then there was his dress. He wore an immaculate black suit, white shirt, and black aviators. A real look from a movie-type deal. So I peered out at this guy with curiosity and he didn't fill up the car. No gas is needed! Instead, he walked with that precision towards my store. He possessed an elegant movement that wasted no energy. As he moved without friction, his aura was one of absolute focus, that was how I felt about it, anyway. He had an uncanny purpose. No one else was in the car, I checked, just him.

In a blink, he was in front of me at the desk.

"Do you need something? directions?" I found myself saying nervously. I didn't want to say directly: "You're not from here, I can tell". I held back on that.

He removed his sunglasses. I wasn't sure if it was out of respect until that was confirmed with a bow.

As I took in his face, I felt an unnatural shudder, a sixth sense, a gut instinct, if you will. It may seem strange, but it felt that this meeting was fated, part of my destiny.

There was a menace there. I quickly studied him, searching my mind as if somehow, I knew him, maybe from a game of cards, but my mind drew a blank.

Then he bowed and presented his card to me; above the personal contact details, it read.

Mr. Katra-San

Mr. Takeshi's Personal Representative and Adviser

I froze. My gut was right. I have only felt fear like this once before in my life.

Bonsai

That name! Until I shared his name with you earlier, "Takeshi-San," I had long since buried it in the deepest vaults of my memory and shared it with no one. Not even a single utterance.

"You are Bonsai, of course," he said.

I simply nodded cautiously.

Had he sent him to kill me? I had never met one, but he looked like a "hitman," at least the type I had seen in movies. As you can imagine, my mind was all over the place. What a week, I thought. It was only a few days ago a couple of locals had come to my store to hustle me. I knew from this man's demeanor any resistance here would be ten times more foolish. All I could do was listen, as I froze to the spot as he explained the reason for his visit, which he delivered clinically.

"I am here with instructions from my boss, Mr. Takeshi-San, whom I believe you know. These are of utmost importance to him. His instruction was that I was to travel from Japan to deliver this invitation in person, which, of course, I am doing presently."

He did not wait for a response. He pulled his hand inside his suit jacket with the precision of a man who could use that hand to swat a fly in the blink of an eye or even kill a man. I thought at that point about running, but in a second, he was handing me an envelope, so pristine it could have been from the President himself, despite the fact that it had been in his breast pocket, it was perfectly folded.

With "For Bonsai Only" written on the front with above it "the House of Takeshi" crest.

I took it from his hand and simply held it hanging in the air as I had just been served papers by some kind of divorce lawyer.

Then, his tone was an octave lighter but still robotic, business-like, and professional.

"Mister Takeshi-San has something to ask of you. He knows you will not let him down. He holds you in high regard".

My mind scrambled, and I tried to think what he might be asking of me, a meeting with Lily? "He knows:" was my immediate thought. But if it is a meeting with Lily he wants, a man like that would equally know I was presently useless to broker such an introduction to my estranged daughter.

He went on, "Please read the contents of the invitation at your leisure. He presumes you will accept. I simply request you contact me on the number on the card I have given. A text is perfectly acceptable with a simple "Yes" or "No" will suffice;" There seemed to be some kind of undertone that I interpreted as a menace, "there will be consequences" otherwise, at least that is what I heard him say.

Then he added with a lighter tone," But as I have said, my boss is very trusting that you will accept". I know you are a very busy man, so I will take no more of your time, Bonsai-San. On behalf of Mister Takeshi-San, with gratitude, I do hope you will accept".

Then, adding, in a slightly complicit tone, like we were coworkers like he was sharing compassionately what he thought was the right thing to do;

"For your sake, may I say, this is a once-in-a-lifetime opportunity. Good Day, Sir:" he said as a farewell and as smoothly as he had arrived, he had vanished again from Salinas in his Toyota Corolla hire car.

"Of course, trembling slightly, I immediately closed the store and retreated here to my den. Like now, I had a scotch to steady my nerves. I am not embarrassed to say a tumbler full that went down the hatch in one gulp. Here is the invitation, Monty," I said and handed my friend the open envelope.

Monty carefully removed the invitation from the envelope like it was an antique already. He could feel the wait of the high-grade cardstock paper in his fingers like a Royal wedding invitation. He carefully read the words on the card;

"Bonsai. Mister Takeshi-San will be playing in the Monterey

Sandy Nicolson

Pro-Am on the 15th of January. It would be the highest honor to Takeshi-San if you would be his personal driver and caddy for the week. Once he hears of your acceptance, more details of the precise arrangements will be made available to you. As a personal note, Mister Takeshi-San would like to express his gratitude in advance for your consideration and trusting acceptance of this offer, for which rest assured, it will be very much worth your while after all these years".

Monty read the words of the invitation twice and then carefully returned the invitation to the envelope and returned it.

He looked at me like I just hit an uncharacteristically good golf shot, an incredulous look, like, in a way, he was proud I had bottled up such complexity until now. It was like he had just opened a can of soda that fizzed everywhere unexpectedly, and he had just been hoping for a simple drink that was now impossible.

We sat in silence for a moment, and the Captain tried to process these truly extraordinary events. Ironically, I hadn't yet either, but I was strangely relieved for the moment that I had shared them. It felt therapeutic. He clasped his hands in thought, like in prayer. Then it was clear it was truly too much detail for even the Captain to process straight away. So he said simply, "You know I have a ticket for that ProAm," and laughed somewhat reluctantly like he was unsure whether to bring any levity to the situation or not.

Bonsai

I smiled, and somehow, we were back to the beginning of our relationship. Where we spoke only with sparse words and left most things unsaid. Life is too complex sometimes, the silence said. "Let's just play golf," our introduction to each other had said right from the start. So, I knew I had shared enough for today and switched gears to ordering him a cab home for the evening.

"Are you going to accept?" he said succinctly.

And all I could say was, "I haven't made up my mind, or I even have an option. But this conversation has helped me move forward towards one. So, thank you."

When the yellow cab swept out into the black night, I sat in my chair and made myself a nightcap. I felt some sort of burden, at least partly, had been lifted from my mind a little. I looked at the invite and the thought returned to me when I first opened the envelope and digested its contents. I smiled. Just maybe, maybe I would get to see her again. The thought was so overwhelming as if her ghost had suddenly joined me in the garage, walking in from a cornfield outside, as if by magic. Just maybe, and whilst there was that chance, how could I say anything but yes to Takeshi? The alternative was he was coming to kill me, but I knew I would already be dead if that is what he wanted, and besides, for all intents and purposes, I might as well be dead given the vacuous life I was leading, so what did I have to lose? I would accept.

Chapter 8

Lauren Is Not Happy About Her Golf Assignment

"Golf, that horrendously boring misogynistic sport middle-aged men play? Seriously, what the heck?"

I had a pretty good relationship with my Section Officer, Blake, my boss. You had to have a pretty sarcastic sense of humor to work as an undercover cop in San Francisco. Otherwise, sometimes, at least, the job would drive you crazy. You realized that from the first stiff, a corpse, a recently departed victim you saw on a job or "dead dolls," as I called them. Their eyes are like empty shells or marbles, lips purple and grotesquely trying to scream something at you, their flesh turning to plastic, bodies in positions they could never achieve in life, even if they practiced yoga, you get the idea. No, if you couldn't let that imprint in your mind turn into something comedic and cartoonish, you were going to be toast. You wouldn't last a minute on the street. So that gives you a little context as to why the dialogue with my boss was sarcastic, dark and edgy always. We had both seen a lot of crap and had grown to realize a certain level of humor to stay sane. In this particular case, I was getting a brief on a new assignment that involved golf for goodness sake. Golf? So, I knew my boss, a white middle-aged guy, played golf, and so I was just messing with him.

"Yes, Lauren, that's right, that's the very one! The sport where we dress like court jesters and chase a white ball around with a stick, sure, you've had your coffee this morning! The sport where it's perfectly acceptable for heterosexual men to give each other a stroke;" he stopped to laugh at his own joke, a sort of embarrassed short chuckle, which was his habit, which I actually found quite endearing. I let him move on with what he was saying about the brief for the job; what was the suspected crime, who was the perp, what we had to do and what he wanted from me was still to come.

"So, seriously, yes, the very sport is golf. It's a big deal in the Bay Area and especially in Monterey Country. They have some of the best courses there. Anyway, they have one where there is a competition every year that brings together professionals and amateur celebrities. When I say celebrities, there are actors and singers and sports stars. Flip me. I wouldn't recognize any of them. I don't mean their Z-list. It's more that I don't keep up, you know, *with that stuff*. Then they also have entrepreneurs and leaders of industry who mostly give money to charity to feel like they're celebrities most likely. You know, the ones that really lie about their handicaps, if you know what that is. Anyway, you get the picture".

"I think I know what you're talking about. No surprise. My father loved the sport. Hence my unhealthy hatred for it". Of course, my boss knew exactly who my father was. So he ignored my petulant comment, which I was thankful for. I felt embarrassed at its lack of maturity. Yes, let's move on, my silence said.

"Well, there is an interesting honey trap we set for a guy attending this year's tournament with the help of leadership. Actually, it wasn't any more complicated than when we got this so-called "corporate guy" an invite to play, but I'll get to that in more detail. Let me pull up some slides I have put together for the brief for you;" he said, and with that, it brought a large screen on the wall in the room to life.

Now, as Blake fires up his slides, let me pause to insert some irony here. So, as you can imagine, there is not a building in San Francisco that is labeled "white collar crime unit". It's just an innocuous building (I can't tell you where obviously), but it's an incredible vanilla office building in downtown San Francisco. It's not like the movies with some flash digital-enabled entrances or false doors or secret floors. Sure, the security is tight, but it's ostensibly just a boring office block. Sure, it's no dump, we have a nice canteen that would compete with a tech company maybe. I've never been to one, but I have no complaints about the food. But in other words, the building itself is incredibly boring, just like Lily's law office. The meeting rooms, like the one I am sitting in right now, are no different. A boardroom-style table, office seating that type of typical furniture and a large screen on the wall for presentations like

Bonsai

the one I was presently receiving. The difference between the gray corporate neighbors in this trendy neighborhood? The cool bit that motivated someone like me to do this job? Well, it wasn't any of the real estate. You know me by now. No, it was the content of the presentation my boss was about to present.

It's the content that drives our game. By "game", I mean our daily fight on the street to fight crime by all means at our disposal. That's what distinguishes things here from a civilian job. It's the way that content translates into action that makes a job like this so exciting for me. Whilst we have an office, it is not an office job. More than that (and I wouldn't indulge my boss with this) but, it inspired and drove me every day. Anyway, enough of my keen bean chat which I only share with you to set the scene. But it's funny how some careers start full of vim and excitement, and some peak and for some, the source of the kicks change. In Blake's case, sure, he was a big boss now, but he was off the street, a desk jockey now but brilliant at strategy. In the Happy Hours, folks would share how he was a badass on the streets once upon a time, maybe he lost his nerve, maybe he got bored, maybe he had to climb the ladder to pay the bills, maybe he had a wasted dream to work in one of those safe corporate jobs where he could present like this every day of the week albeit with much more mundane content, I genuinely wasn't sure, but I was sure I liked working with him and boy could he tell the story behind every op.

Anyway, back to his presentation.

His first slide was a picture of an old Japanese guy, who might have been handsome once, titled "Takeshi-San". A peculiar mismatch between an old cracked face and hair that was from a younger man (and I am not saying it was dyed). It was just the part of his face that belonged to a much younger man. His striking feature if you like. In a quick summary, for now, the other thing was his eyes that pierced like a surgeon good at making the precise diagnosis of his patient before getting to work with his knife.

"Do you know who he is?" Blake quizzed me.

"An old Japanese guy with good hair and sharp eyes!" I said sarcastically.

"In a nutshell, he is a "Yakuza". In our terms, a mob boss."

"Don't you think some things sound so much better in other languages?"

"Sure, and Yakuza is named after a card game, sort of like blackjack. Don't ask how I know that. Anyway, I don't need to give you a complete history lesson here, the relevant part is that his father sent him to live with family here in San Francisco when he was 12 in 1939, just as the Second World War broke out to avoid him going to the army, who knows how but he was smuggled in, as you couldn't immigrate from Japan then. Three years later, he was caught up in the internship of the Japanese in 1942 in Japantown after the bombing of Pearl Harbor".

"Come on, this is a history lesson, but candidly, it saves me googling later," I said with a smile as I scooped a handful of trail mix I had just opened on the conference table and laid out in front of me like bird seed.

"The internships were basically where they were rounded up and put in detention centers until after the war. That is where he built his gang, or in today's terms, built his first network. As I say, he had immigrated first through Hawaii family contacts illegally, of course, and then to San Francisco. I'm not a smart ass. This is all proudly on his Wikipedia entry (not the gang boss reference, of course). It wasn't until the 1950's he was allowed to be naturalized. What's not recorded is that between his release from internship and the 1950s, he had lived on his guile and contacts in Japan to build a pretty sizable drug dealing business that by his time of naturalization he had turned into a legitimate business transporting agricultural equipment originally to Salinas and by the 1960s, he was quite the entrepreneur, he turned that into a Transpacific transportation business. At its core his enterprise was a cover for American guns traded by American GIs brought back from Vietnam sold to him, and fortunately for them, he was bringing amphetamines the other way, and so most often, there was the perfect barter. That was the start of the boom in legitimate Japanese imports to the US, you know, mopeds, cars, electronics. Ultimately, those shipping containers were making it every which way for him".

"Not being rude, but are we going to make it to the next slide?" I said, taking my last mouthful of trail mix and quickly adding, "Sorry I am being flippant. This is interesting stuff".

Ignoring me as usual, he went on," Don't worry, I will bring you right up to speed in no time! It's a good job. You're good at arresting people, Lauren:" and with that said, he clicked the PowerPoint forward.

At this point, I suddenly felt nauseous. I thought I was going to vomit the trail mix across the table. On the next slide, there was a woman who was the complete doppelganger of Lily! My mind raced. Blake had never met Lily. In fact, I don't think I had ever told him about her. Before I could say, "Is this a big joke? Why do you have a picture of my girlfriend on this deck?" He said sincerely, "Is something wrong? Do you know her? You look ill?" I realized this was maybe some awful coincidence, and he was messing me around, so I replied, "No, maybe the trail mix was funky. Go on, please. Who is she?"

"Well, this is an old photograph. It took a lot to get it from Homeland Security records. This is Ly Takeshi. We suspect she was a Vietnamese prostitute he married and imported, so to speak, in

Bonsai

1973. From her immigration forms, she was a lot younger than him. She was 25 in 1973, and he was 49. The dirty old man".

I was still a little spellbound. "No, it couldn't be," my mind was racing. My hands were "clamming up", my tongue was really dry, and I had dead eyes, and my feet were stuck to the floor like they had been suddenly magnified.

"Are you sure you are okay?" Blake said, "You need water, Lauren?"

"I was just thinking the same, dirty old man. She is very attractive and innocent-looking," I said in an explanation to move us along.

"Really?" Blake said, taking a second look, "I think she looks a little plain to me. Not my type."

I resisted the urge to say something mean to Blake. Like "she looks identical to my girlfriend, and I think she is the most attractive girl in the world. You idiot!" I didn't say anything, though, but my heart rate had increased twenty percent.

"Anyway, for a short time, they lived here in Pebble Beach," Blake clicked to the next slide;" so this is the house present day, not then, but he still owns it, well one of his affiliated companies, to be exact. I have always wondered who lives in those houses. Anyway, since around 1980, it's been a ghost ship, so to speak. Takeshi went back to Japan on a "business trip" in 1979 and was arrested for tax evasion. He served only a year. As always, guys like that have good lawyers. A year was a joke. Anyway, as much as his legitimate businesses continued to grow into a fairly massive conglomerate, he never returned to the US, and strangely, his wife, Ly, stayed on in the US for the year he was inside, living in that 8-bedroom house in Pebble Beach. Then roughly at the time he was released, she returned to Japan never to return ".

"Children? Did they have children?" I asked with my best detective eyes.

"No, not here, not then. Maybe he was too old".

"Anyway, the State commissioned a study last year to look at deregulating the gaming industry in California. I won't bore you, but it's a big thing Nationally following a Supreme Court Case that says that the constitution permits gaming...."

"I bet you're a big Jeopardy fan, Blake!"

"Anyway, as part of the study, they were assessing how much the current illegitimate gambling market was worth. You know, so the State could work out if they legalized it, how much would they stand to make? They started pulling stray pieces of wool, so to speak, as they did their research. These were a bunch of economists, geeks, not cops. Arguably, they did a better job with their study than, present company excluded, most undercover cops would do".

"That is because most of them are gamblers," I interjected smartly.

"Well, these guys, mostly young economists, played poker in Japantown, underground dens. Probably too green to understand how dangerous that was. But as they mapped it all out, they realized a security company owned by a company that led all the way to Takeshi Industries was the one that moved the cash. Smart guys, those economists, but really, this wasn't that complicated, just a kid economist smoking a cigarette in the street in the middle of a game of poker. He has obviously watched too many movies and wrote down the food delivery van's registration, and well, we went from there. Anyway, suffice to say they were smart enough to know this was hot and brought it into us".

"But if he was so clean until these brainiacs worked out what they did, why has he never returned to California? Sounds like a case closed. We have an extradition treaty with Japan, don't we? So, he was never really safe in Japan?"

"Maybe, but these guys, you know, they have a lot of power and going down the extradition treaty route takes time, and it trips too many people to tip him off. But you know it is strange he never returned after the tax case".

"Maybe, but maybe there is something else. Something personal. A Vietnamese rival? One of the Triads in Chinatown?"

"Even if it's gang rivalry, at that level, that's just geography. Those guys are all multinational organizations".

"Hmm;" my detective skills had hit a roadblock.

The next picture was of a man in his mid-twenties in an immaculate suit and plain white shirt. A handsome Japanese man with perfect angular features. The sort of guy who would play a stereotypical assassin in a Hong Kong gangster movie.

The title of the slide was "Takeshi-San - Personal Representative and Adviser".

"Let me come back to the relevance of this guy. I said earlier, with a lot of help from senior leadership, I won't bore you with what it took. Anyway, a line about better Asian representation or something worked. We got Takeshi, a golf nut, an invite to the Pro-Am tournament in Monterey. We took a gamble, if you excuse the pun, and figured

a. nearly 30 years had passed since he had left the US and, so whatever stopped him from coming back may have passed.

b. We, or rather, I figured he likely has a massive ego like all these types of guys and

c. Did I say he is a golf nut?

and last he is getting old, and this is a last-chance type of thing? Anyway, suffice it to say he took the bait and accepted the invite. Pretty smart, huh?

In fact, we got one of the greatest golfers to deliver the invite personally. Guess what, he accepted".

"Ha, you're a genius, Blake".

"Anyway, back to this guy. This special representative guy flew to San Francisco the other week, and naturally, we tracked him. And we wanted to know why he was here? And so the breadcrumbs led us to the next slide. So loyal, btw he rented a Toyota Camry. Anyway," and he hit the next slide.......

At this point, when I combined the picture of the Lily look alike and the gas station in Salinas I was now looking at, I was really freaking out. Was this gas station owner Lily's dad? It seemed far-fetched. But in my job, and maybe because of my upbringing, I have seen so many things that my version of far-fetched may be different from yours. No offense.

I didn't know everything about Lily's childhood, but I did know when she got drunk and wanted to show off about how far she had come to make it to Stanford, to make it to the law firm, to make to the youngest Partner that she would wax on about the crap hole gas station she and her "awful" father ran in Salinas. Maybe the last independent gas station in Salinas. Her Dad was a real "Willy Loman" character from an Arthur Miller play she would say patronizingly, knowing that plays were not my thing. A salesman that didn't change with the times or something, stubbornly, she explained. He should have sold the gas station years ago. I didn't really listen to her explanation. She was obviously making a point of her intellectual superiority over me. Making a point that she was a hero because she was a true underdog that defied the odds and, second, trying to make her whole life passage to date somehow hold a higher intellectual standing by attaching that literary reference. She was trying to give her life some much-needed gravitas and, in contrast, making the point that I was over privileged and had everything given to me. She was so insecure, but I loved her regardless.

All I could really think about was how many crappy gas stations there could be in Salinas. Independent ones, that is. And maybe most importantly, I knew her mother had disappeared. In fact, she never knew her. Wow, really? Surely not? I know there is serendipity, but this is too much, is it not? I must get more sleep. This can't be real, I said to myself.

As he flipped to the next slide, I didn't even read the title card or really tune in to what my boss was now saying by way of explanation, something like, "This is the gas station owner. He runs it on his own".

"There was no one else there when Takeshi's man paid the visit. So this is the only person he went to see. He didn't fill up with gas and exchanged a few words, and presented this guy with an envelope, our surveillance guys reported.

But get this, Takeshi has remarkably registered this guy as his caddy for the event......sure the guy plays amateur golf in the area with a retired army guy, it seems, but surely that doesn't qualify him to caddy for one of the wealthiest men in Japan......"

I couldn't focus on all of my boss's research he was detailing now.

It was Lily's Dad, no question about it. It was him. I had never seen his picture, but I knew in my gut this was him. I was sure of it.

A cold sweat ran down my back, and I thought my life was turning into some kind of weird movie. I couldn't control my thought processes and the connections I was making here.

All I could do was look at his face. The face was in complete contrast to Takeshi's. His face looked too old for his body. His face had two of the saddest eyes I have seen, in contrast to Takeshi. He looked like a walking ghost.

Sandy Nicolson

I leaned in a little, extra curious for obvious reasons to understand the full story this face told. The part of the story that Lily held back on. She was too one-sided for her father to really be as much of a deadbeat as she said. He may have run a gas station in the sticks, but he had a super bright daughter who, for all her insecurities and things that bugged me sometimes, the "light" nickname she got from work was unfair. To me, she was the light of my life and in this perverse way, I got to meet her father for the first time, and if Darwin was to be believed and the former prostitute was her mother, there must be a lot more to these parents than meets the eye.

I gathered my wits. Get a grip, I told myself, get tough Lauren. I didn't want to draw too much attention to my focus, so I simply told Blake to go back through the slides slowly from the start, which he did, and I got one more good look at Ly. And sure enough, she was the spit of Lily.

I shook my head and imagined myself in a cold shower to settle my nerves. I took a breath.

"What do you want me to do then? I think I roughly get where we have got to. The big boss guy is coming to the event, and we get a chance to nail him.

"Well, sure, obviously, we want to arrest Takeshi and bring him in. On US soil, we don't have years for extradition treaties. On top of that, Takeshi has cancer. He is dying.

Bonsai

His private plane is going to land at Monterey Airport this weekend. You will get the details. The old gas station owner used to be his driver. So, we expect he may be his transport. Real James Bond odd job set up with that guy?"

"James Bond?"

"You haven't seen Goldfinger?"

"What age do you think I am?"

"Anyway, here is the thing. Getting the honeytrap set up, like I said, involved some very senior leadership. Connected people. This isn't an ordinary event. Probably one of the most prestigious golf events in the world that he is playing at. So, the quid pro quo for getting him here with securing the Willy Wonka ticket is he needs to play the tournament through to the finish, and we can't arrest him on the course in front of the cameras".

"Seriously, these mysterious leadership people know he's a crook?"

"It's all about appearances and not disrupting a bunch of geopolitical stuff. Way above my pay grade. They know nothing of the details I have shared with you, and in return, I have nothing on the bigger picture.

All l know is our God asked their God to make sure he was invited, and our God is obviously on our side of the fence. Government, in other words. So, their God said, "I don't need or want to know why, but one condition is if we do invite him, he plays, you make darn sure there is no funny business on the course. Nothing for the media in other words". Our God knows that there didn't need to be an:" or else" that was an unspoken given".

"What do you mean by "or else"?"

"Lauren, of all people, you know. I don't need to tell you what the world turns on. Budgets depend on respecting these types of things".

That was one of the only times Blake made me cringe. I hated this type of politics he was implying.

I, of course, knew what he was inferring. At that moment, for the last fraction of a second, I thought I should confess to my boss why I was the wrong person for this job for so many reasons. But as I thought about it, I was in too deep already, and not least, whichever way this turned out was not going to be good for Lily. For all our squabbles, I still loved her and as I thought about this case, my lies to Lily about my profession, how much this could hurt her in so many ways. No, the more I thought about the right thing to do, the more I realized that I had more than the duty I had sworn to when I accepted this job and swore allegiance.

I had a duty to Lily, too.

Chapter 9

Are You Ready For The Tournament, Bonsai?

And so, the Pro-Am and, therefore, Takeshi's visit was two weeks away when I played my last game with the Captain. We played Poppy Hills, a longish course, so I was thankful the Captain accepted my proposition that we rent a cart.

Our round was just like the old days, our conversation was strictly business, e.g. we kept it to our game. But after the round, and as if it was pre-planned, he asked if I wanted a drink on the 19th.

"Time for one of those Laphroiag's."

With all the craziness of the last few weeks, he didn't need to ask twice.

We found a space on the deck away from the busy Friday afternoon foot traffic by the bar. I got the drinks, and there was already a noticeable buzz at the bar about the upcoming ProAm. I could overhear folks next to me as I ordered our scotches.

They were a couple, maybe husband and wife, who knows, in their 40s but filled with the excitement of a couple of teenagers at the upcoming event. They were sharing notes on the professionals who were signed up to play in the event. Apparently, some of the best players in the world were going to be playing this year. I hadn't even checked who.

They talked about who they were going to follow around. I can't remember precisely the questions they were asking of each other, but they were questions like;

Who was in form from recent events?

How would playing with an amateur impact the play of the professionals?

Would it put the professional off if the amateur was playing lousy?

Who would you want to be paired with if you were famous or vice versa if you were a professional golfer?

Even the projected weather forecast was being debated the wife immediately studying her smartphone at the prompt of her husband.

In other words the type of detailed questions that only comes from being a passionate fan of anything. But hearing the rapid-fire questions instantly terrified me and somehow broke me from a dream I had been living in since I was asked to caddy for Takeshi. The dangerous man whose wife I had an affair with 30 years ago. No ordinary man but a Yakuza, a feared and hard-nosed businessman. A man whose wife's child, my child, I had raised to adulthood on my own whilst running a gas station in Salinas. A man who thirty years later was coming to play in a famous golf tournament that would be televised, and his returning swan song was to ask me, this otherwise down-on-his-luck gambler and high handicap golfer, to be his caddy. I suddenly felt dizzy and filled with terror. Could I really do all this? Was I mentally prepared for all of these unknowns?

I was ecstatic when the barmaid finally broke me from my anxious state when I heard her ask me (for the third time, apparently) if I was going to pay.

When I found the Captain at the table, he saw the terror on my face instantly and, of course, didn't need to ask why, but instead, he said with humor, "Your golf wasn't that bad today, no really;" and then gave me a comforting smile.

After letting me gather my thoughts by watching a group take their money's worth with putts on the 18th, our table overlooked, the Captain finally spoke.

"First things first, I know a guy that has trained some of the best caddies in the world. A former marine who moved here about the same time as me. A solid man. I have arranged for him to spend time with you this week. Teach you "the way," as they say.

He joked that for this man, it would be no different from

when he was in the field in the special forces, and he had to train a group of untrained villagers how to defend themselves from attack. Besides, you can't make love to another man's wife and then make him look bad at golf. I know what's worse!"

The Captain's levity made me smile, and I took a sip of Laphroaig and toasted him for his thoughtfulness.

"Thank you. I don't know how I could repay you!"

"Well, I don't plan on selling my Camry before I die, and I dare say it might need fixing it again".

The Captain, having covered his first agenda point, got quickly to the next with military precision, so we didn't dwell, was my guess.

"So, help me understand a little more of what we covered the other night. I don't mean to pry, so don't answer if you don't want to, but I don't like trying to sleep at night with questions I don't know the answer to or rather want to know the answers to".

"Sure," I said, "ask me anything you want to".

"Well, give me a little more context on how you got here and mixed up with this Takeshi guy".

I was pleased he didn't ask about Ly yet. I wasn't quite ready for that since I came back down to this reality of sorts, it was relief

Bonsai

from listening to the bar side conversation and the daunting few days that lay ahead. What the Captain had asked for, I could cover first. I could handle that.

"So my grandparents were poor farm laborers in Korea in the early 20th century. We don't need to go into the what's what, but Korea was in a rough spot then, and they were poor. The Methodist church missionaries found their community and offered a chance for my Uncle, a young man, a bright, strong young man, to come and work on their plantation in Hawaii. My father, to his fault, was offered too but refused. My Uncle was a good worker, and in turn, they transferred him to the mainland USA around the time of the First World War, when there was an agriculture boom to feed the troops in Europe. He moved to Salinas, where he settled".

"So your people were originally like slaves of a sort, like my people? I didn't know that," the Captain interjected.

I nodded and continued the story.

"Then serendipitously, my Uncle met Takeshi, who at the time had a legitimate business. His first, transporting agricultural equipment from San Francisco to Salinas. The story goes that he met Takeshi in a saloon downtown in Salinas and they hit it off because my Uncle could speak Japanese and had spent time like Takeshi in Hawaii. They drank whiskey and talked all night about the men they had seen "walking on water" in Hawaii without a care in the world.

Takeshi offered him a job as a driver. What started out as a fairly mundane job (but better than being a laborer) driving agricultural products back and forth between San Francisco and Salinas soon evolved as Takeshi's business interests continued to diversify. Soon, my Uncle became Takeshi's personal driver. "Behind great wealth is usually a crime," so as you can imagine, not every interest Takeshii had was legitimate".

"Don't worry, I am listening," said the Captain as he was presently calculating the pair's scorecard for their game on the table in front of them with a short pencil.

"Anyway, my Uncle was his driver until 1975, so for 20 years. At that point, my Uncle's emphysema got really bad (he was a heavy smoker), and in those days, no one knew smoking was bad for you. For his loyalty, Takeshi asked him what he wanted, I guess by way of a retirement gift.

My Uncle asked for two simple things from Takeshi. This is roughly what he said;

"As you know, my nephew is back home in Seoul, in the Gyeonggi province. He works hard as a mechanic. He is not an exceptionally bright boy, but oil is in both of our veins. But in his father's veins there was junk, too many war memories he wanted to disappear. I would like a visa for my nephew to come to California and work with me here. Second, all I ask for is a simple garage near

Monterey. Where me and my nephew can work on your cars, Takeshi-San.

"That is all you ask?" Takeshi had said, touched by his friend's modesty.

My Uncle was no entrepreneur. Once upon a time, gas stations were good businesses, something my Uncle knew something about, and he wouldn't have to move far to work. Plus, he would be right back next to the fields. The fields he used to work with his hands as a young man. Romantic, in a way, I guess. Believe it or not, once upon a time, that garage of mine was a decent business of sorts.

Anyway, in addition to the garage, his second wish was granted, and I received a US Visa.

When I arrived, Takeshi was splitting his time between Japan and the US, and he needed a new driver. I was vouched for by my Uncle, so my selection was obvious. I could split my time with the garage as, by that point, Takeshi was only really in the Bay Area for golf trips and the occasional business meeting in Japantown in San Francisco.

So, for a while me and my Uncle had a great life. I drove Takeshi in his Mercedes 600 Limo and helped out in the garage when Takeshi was overseas, and my Uncle managed to run the garage. Despite all the things happening in the world in the 1970's, we lived in somewhat of a bubble in that garage in those days.

But a distraction slowly crept into my life. In late 1975, Takeshi asked me to pick up his wife from San Francisco Airport. I remember every detail of that day. It was the day I met her. The day I met Ly for the first time.

I had no idea what to expect. I just held a sign at arrivals; "Mrs Takeshi" in Japanese.

When a girl close to my age was introducing herself in very basic English as Mrs Takeshi, I struggled to take it in, to process it, not because I doubted it was her. More because it was love at first sight. Believe it or not, that happens.

She had these mercurial eyes that told a million stories of untold lives. They sparkled black like anthracite. It was like she had lived for a million years. She was doll-like in her complexion. Her red lipstick was perfectly painted. Her jet-black hair was held tight in a ponytail. She wore this perfect silk kimono, black with a cherry blossom print:"

I noticed the Captain's tumbler was empty and was conscious I was taking a trip down memory lane. Plus, it was getting late.

"Sorry, Captain, I am probably sharing too much detail. It's

Bonsai

probably that I have carried this history sealed shut inside my tank for a lifetime. Anyway, I see you're out of oil. Let me get you a refill. Maybe one for the road?" referring to his empty glass.

"No, I want to understand the pieces. This is an interesting story, more to come, it seems. It's my round, I'll go," and he rose to his feet, "by the way, you shot 78. It's the best I have seen you play. These developments have lit a fire in you;" he handed me the scorecard.

"I'll keep it more snappy when you get back. The most important thing is around that time. Takeshi was arrested in Japan and spent a year in jail. That is where the trouble started. I will tell you about that when you return".

"Sounds like that's where the interesting bit starts," he said mischievously. He smiled warmly as he left the table.

I turned my gaze to a husband and wife (I presumed) playing the 18th. The couple, I guessed, were about my age. I looked on ruefully, they looked like they were blissfully happy. I sentimentally thought they had likely been married a long time. They had a couple of children who had graduated college, most likely. Maybe a few grandchildren. They likely all got together for the perfect Christmas. The type of idyllic family get-togethers that were portrayed in department store television adverts. A life I would never have.

Sandy Nicolson

What if we had been like that, Ly and I, a regular couple, playing together chasing the sunset in Pebble Beach? I was suddenly melancholic and felt the air cooling. The setting sun glowed red as it sank behind the green.

Chapter 10

Takeshi Is On His Way, And Bonsai Remembers How He Met Ly

I stood in my den the morning of the pick-up dressed in my one and only suit, a simple white shirt and my Crockett and Jones shoes. I had polished them to oblivion over the course of the previous week since the invitation had arrived. It had been a long time since I had worn a suit. I must have worn it since, but all I could think of was my Uncle's funeral. I couldn't remember another time for some reason. Maybe there hadn't been. I was just glad that moths or similar beasties hadn't eaten it. There were no holes as far as I could see.

As I drove my old Ford to the shed to pick up the car, all I could think about was her and that other time, which felt like a surreal dream world. But maybe that wasn't another time, but you know, the whole time? My whole world felt like a dream now.

I couldn't help but reminisce about the old times and the prospect of driving the old car again.

The first time, and every time after, I would look at her in the rearview mirror. I drove on autopilot most of the days that she had been in the car. I was, what you might say, sort of mesmerized by her.

Sandy Nicolson

She was like an exotic bird that had flown in and sat in the back seat of the limousine. It was as if she found herself detached from her natural habitat and found herself in mine. That vulnerability amplified her attraction.

Every time I drove her, she spent the whole journey looking out of the limo window as if taking notes of Monterey County and secretly planning her escape. I presumed she was taking in the similarities and differences of the South Bay and Japan. Whenever I dropped her back at the house, her expression notably changed. I realized that the look in her eyes then was not a fear of her new country but of Takeshi and maybe what would happen to her if she did indeed try and escape.

I could sense that she noticed I was watching a lot of the time, and she didn't seem to mind. In fact, she encouraged it. I thought she wanted me to admire her beauty, but I think she was really trying to figure out how much of a Takeshi man I was. Anyway, we both coexisted in the cage, so to speak, in those early times.

Then came the moment. Not all of us can point to one singular point in time that changed our lives. For some, there are too many points, and for others, it's just too hard to say. For me, there is no doubt it was the time Takeshi invited me to his study and poured me a whiskey in the fall of 1979. It was the one and only

Bonsai

time he did that. Usually, I would sit in the service quarters and wait for my instructions on where Ly wanted to drive that particular day.

I had sat in a seat at his command, a seat way too big for me. I instantly drowned in it.

I tried not to look out of the study window at the panorama that was the golf hole at Pebble Beach, the house overlooked, and the Pacific Ocean beyond. I had no idea why he had summoned me. This had never happened before, and my mind raced. It must be a good thing, I kept telling myself. He sat on the side of his desk, nursing his own whiskey, looking down at me and said, "I am going to Japan today, which you know about, of course, because you will drive me to the airstrip. What you don't know is that I am going to ask you the most important request, one man can ask another. There is no higher request, except perhaps maybe in relation to a child, which I do not have. I am going to ask you to take care of my wife while I am gone."

There had been something extra in his emphasis of "take care" and "while I am gone" that days later when I learned of his arrest, hung around me like a stubborn Monterey fog. I could not make sense of it. Why would such a successful and senior man ask his lowly driver to take care of his most prized possession, if you will? If I am honest, I was also a little perturbed about how he seemed to know he would be "gone" and for some uncalculated amount of time. I instantly felt a great responsibility, probably the greatest of my life, with this commission.

As I recalled the pivotal moment, presently, from all those years ago, I joined the 101 and headed North to the airport junction where the Shed was. As I did so, I passed the sign for the Pacific Grove turn-off.

Lovers Point in Pacific Grove is where we would go for our first walks, or in retrospect, they were dates. We didn't call them these or even recognize them as such. Lovers Point, if you have never heard of it, is an outpost of rocks in a pretty but sleepy town called Pacific Grove. The rocks reach out towards the Pacific, which crashes up around them, most of the time, like a friendly dog, and in April when we first started our meets, with pink and purple ice plants, which create a magical pink carpet effect. And guess what? The scene is surrounded by Cyprus Trees. If you google them, to see what they look like, I think you will agree they look like large Bonsai trees. Well, that is at least what Ly thought they looked like when she first saw them and from then on, that is what she called me affectionately; "Bonsai".

We would go early in the morning when no one was around. At first, I thought it was because I thought she was ashamed to be seen with me, but as I got to know her, I realized it was because she was being romantic, and she loved that we had it all to ourselves.

Bonsai

Like in those moments, the earth felt like it belonged just to us or maybe the occasional otter or a pod of dolphins that would sometimes swim by as the sun rose.

It wasn't straight away that I realized that our feelings were reciprocal. After I dropped Takeshi off at his plane, I returned to the House to present myself at her service. When I got there, I was told by the housekeeper that she was in the rose garden. I found my way there through something of a labyrinth garden that Takeshi had designed. She was dressed in a white dress, like a wedding dress, I had thought, which was perfectly framed by the white roses on a trellis around her. I spoke a little Japanese, so I bowed and told her I was at her service until Takeshi returned to his instruction.

She simply smiled demurely and said simply that she would like me to report every morning at sunrise to take her to Lovers Point in Pacific Grove, and we would walk there before breakfast every day. That was her only wish, at least at that point.

And so, of course, I did as she asked. Typically, there would be no other car in the carpark apart from the Takeshi, a baby blue Mercedes 600 Limo. We would typically walk to the end of the path, where we could look back toward Monterey. We would sit on one of the thousand-year-old stones, with the ocean casting up in front of us.

We did this almost mechanically for a month. Then, one day,

it happened. As we turned toward the car, she simply reached out her hand and put her hand in mine. It was an unusually calm day. The ocean was flat, and the sky was naked blue in anticipation. I didn't resist. In a strange way, it felt like this was a natural extension of my instructions; "to take care of her." Maybe I should have, but I simply didn't question it. Instead, I let our hands accept each other and without words, somehow, we knew we had both accepted something that was inevitable.

In the weeks that followed that simple holding of hands, we carried on our tradition of morning visits to Lover's Point, but in the smallest of increments, with each trip, we got closer to each other and with each trip, it became obvious that Takeshi was not coming home earlier and nothing otherwise seemed destined to get in the way of our fledgling relationship, if you could call it that.

By the time a month had passed when the weather was good, we would huddle on the rocks, and she would giggle, as every so often, the ocean would rise up a little further than we expected and wet our faces. She had the most disarming giggle, the giggle of a child, with an innocence that maybe neither of us deserved. We could sit there for hours, not saying a word, just holding each other's hands and looking West. With each day that passed with our morning ritual, I came to realize, maybe subconsciously, that she was tremendously happy, maybe for the first time in her life. She felt free and, more

Bonsai

specifically, at that time, free of Takeshi and his control.

Every day, the view was slightly different, a cloud placed in a different spot, a new rock exposed, a wave that went a little higher, and a bird unseen before that would swoop in for a morning catch. And now and again, a whale would come up to pay its greetings out there in the Bay. It was an idyllic time.

When the sun rose, I would typically hold an umbrella above her head, like in an old picture.

As mornings came and went, we both began to stay in the park steadily longer, and we would naturally take an interest in other couples. Locals who would, at weekends, lay out travel rugs and set picnics with simple sandwiches, tea and cakes. The fanciest it got was some folks who would bring little BBQs and make tacos. Occasionally, the wind would bring the spice to our noses and then carry it off to sea. So, in time, Ly demanded that we have our own picnics and simple ones, too. She wanted to be just like the others there. So, much to the confusion of the housekeeper and chef used to elaborate requests, they found themselves making simple ham sandwich baskets with apples and a flask of tea for our trips to the shore.

Then, after our picnic lunches, Ly began to get a little bolder still and insisted we go and explore the local shops, which, of course, we did.

Sandy Nicolson

Of course, this idyll wasn't going to last.

By summer, I think we had both forgotten about Takeshi altogether. I presumed he called her regularly. I never asked, and he never contacted me, which, of course, I had no complaints about.

We were both consumed with each other. We had fallen in love. We lived completely in the moment. I am not sure if that is because we didn't want to speak of our past, as neither of us had been in it together and as for the future, well, that was just too scary to contemplate. In all of this head-over-heels stuff, somehow, I forgot that obviously, as Takeshi's wife, she must have had a ruthless side, a part of her that had both led him to her and attracted him. Takeshi, simply, wasn't the kind of guy that either met or was attracted to a "so-called" regular girl. He was clearly a complicated man. Of course, I was in love and didn't give this a thought, not a bit. Instead, when we continued with our theater. I was completely in love.

One day, we went to the Pacific Grove Tourist Center and came out loaded with pamphlets that looked to any passerby like we had just arrived. We looked like a giddy new couple. One of the pamphlets advertised the Pfeiffer Waterfall and the nearby redwood forest trails.

Ly was adamant we must go. I told her she must get flat shoes, and in turn, she told me to organize a simpler car. In other words, not the limo. My task was harder than it sounds. Takeshi had a formidable car collection, and not one of them could be called simple. I concluded that my old Ford truck was simply not good enough for Ly, so after perusing his garage, and this might seem strange. I concluded that an Emerald Green 1970 Porsche 911T would fit the bill. I didn't think for a second that the man who owned it was presently in a Tokyo jail cell, and I was cavorting with his wife and playing with his toys. I am not sure what he meant by "I am going to ask you to take care of my wife" and whether this was what he had meant. I wanted that to be true and was quite happy to believe it unconditionally.

Sandy Nicolson

Chapter 11
How We Made Lily At Pfeiffer Falls

I remember each fragment of the day we went to Pfeiffer Falls and can relive every second of it in a beat, which, of course, I have from my seat many times.

On the day it happened, I picked her up at our usual time just as the sun was rising. The sky was a deep red, and of course, they say a red sky in the morning is a shepherd's warning or something like that. But I wasn't thinking of such superstitions as I pulled into the u-shaped driveway in front of Takeshi's mansion overlooking the Lodge at Pebble Beach in his Porsche 911 to pick up his girl to take her on a picnic for the first time to the Big Sur….maybe I should have been more thoughtful. I honestly don't know what got hold of me. I have never been anywhere as close to as bold as I was that day, any other time in my life. Life, like that car's engine, purred inside of me. I felt alive like never before. It was like Takeshi himself had entered my body and was willing me to enjoy this experience and make it his own.

"Take care of her;" he had said.

As I turned off the purring engine and stepped out of the car, my chest tightened as I looked at the front door opening and saw Ly. Up until that point, she had always worn, at least in my company, perfectly made silk dresses in all manner of designs, and each time, her hair was perfectly held high in a bun or in a strict ponytail. Her makeup was always perfectly painted, like she had a tribe of people help apply it for hours before each meeting. Instead, this morning, as I waited by the Porsche in the driveway, I was completely flummoxed, taken completely off guard, when she appeared at the doorway. What I saw wasn't Ly but someone else, an "American Ly" dressed in Western clothes.

Rather than her usual, elaborate silk dresses, for some reason, on this day, she wore a simple pair of jeans and a white shirt, her hair was undone and hung down to just above her breasts. The shirt was open to just above her chest bone. She was wearing a pair of tan cowboy boots. Her makeup was almost non-existent, and I could see her amazing figure for the first time as the jeans hugged her tight.

She had apparently bought the clothes on one of our shopping trips as I waited outside the store in Pacific Grove. It may seem strange to say this when she was dressed so simply, but she looked incredible.

It wasn't just the clothes. She was wearing an authentic smile that said, at least to me, "I love you, and I have been waiting just for you:" No one before or since has ever looked at me the way she did that day. I forgot completely in that instant that I was a humble

Sandy Nicolson

driver/mechanic and servant to Takeshi and my Uncle. At that moment, I was none of those things, instead, I was ten foot tall, and Ly was my girl.

I moved to help her with the picnic basket she was carrying, which we had bought together one day in Pacific Grove.

The drive to Big Sur was magical. We drove mostly in a beautiful frozen silence, listening to the purr of the perfectly tuned Porsche engine. From the Speedometer, it only had factory miles and had almost certainly never been driven on a public road, or at least not like this. As we crossed Bixby Bridge, I could see Ly looking out at the Pacific, which showed the signs of storms months before. Whitehorses raced chaotically across the scape. It was perhaps a harbinger of things to come. But for today, all you could do was forget about the future, stay in the present, and watch the hungry sun rise up to find its place in the sky.

I could sense her smiling a free, giddy smile in spite of everything. We were both smiling. We were sort of like Bonnie and Clyde, I suppose. Of course, this was all in spite of the inevitable consequences when (not if) Takeshi found out that his driver had overstepped the mark when it came to; "taking care of his wife". If this were to be our last day on earth, then you couldn't eclipse this moment no matter what pain and consequences followed.

In time, that flashed past faster than it should have but, yet leaving a memory that would last a lifetime we were at Pfeiffer Falls, and I carefully parked the Porsche. Despite all the risks I was taking, and may I say again uncharacteristically, for some reason, I suddenly had a fear that I best make sure the car was safe. So, I made sure it was parked under a big Red Oak, off the road, in a little grass meadow.

"Isn't it beautiful;" she said and then spoke a few sentences in Japanese. She spoke for both of us as we took in the falls, which were fully charged, and the water was letting its presence be known on the beach below. As we stood with the picnic basket at our feet, taking in the scene, the morning sun now fully risen, Ly suddenly took my hand forcefully and led me with a tug toward a sign that said, "ENTRY FORBIDDEN". It was like some spirit had entered her being and taken over her soul. In the 6 months or so that I had been her guardian of sorts, I had never seen her act with such abandon. Without asking, she climbed over the sign and stood on the other side of the gate with a childlike smile on her face, testing me. Hypnotized, I followed her and soon, we were both on the other side, headed down a path to the beach below like two children that had skipped school. We had the whole place to ourselves. There was not a sign of another person, and as we walked across the beach, it felt like our footprints on the sand were the first made by a human.

We both walked towards the waterfall, and with each step,

you could sense the intensity, the electricity between us. It shimmered in the light like a thousand crystals falling to earth. It had a mythical quality. If a unicorn had suddenly ridden through it at that precise point, it would not have felt unnatural. Just like the intensity of the ocean in front of us, its power and energy were a continual flow, and the noise it generated, which, of course, grew louder with each step we took toward it, was overwhelming. Our senses were consumed by it. At that moment, there was nothing else in our world. There was a magnet pulling us towards it, whether we wanted to or not. It was our destiny.

We found a cave, maybe 50 meters from the waterfall. Ly laid out a travel rug, and suddenly, as if in a trance, I walked toward her, and we began to kiss. A deep, passionate kiss. A type of kiss I had never experienced. My body was part of hers and her's mine. I don't remember undressing, but when I opened my eyes, we were naked and joined as one. Her eyes looked into mine deeply and seemed to be peering deep within me, into my inner self. I was holding her tighter than I ever held someone, and I could feel her legs around me, she was like some marine animal that had caught me and was tumbling under the ocean, taking me deeper with them, and I wasn't resisting. I couldn't if I wanted to. It was as if, my whole life, I had been destined to be consumed in this way, just like some kind of animal that knows its place in the hierarchy. Her eyes flashed at mine each time we tumbled, and I knew that she loved

Bonsai

me, and so, of course, did I.

I am not sure how long we made love for, maybe an eternity. It felt like we had opened a gate and entered a different parallel time continuum. Every sense in my body was awakened. Finally, we both called loudly to the ocean and collapsed in each other's arms, and the moment was forever frozen in our memories. I knew instantly that there would never be another moment like it. I felt something that had been part of me leave me forever, some sort of passenger I didn't know I was carrying. It left me and joined Ly, never to return in the same form. And then there was the briefest moment of peace, and we just sat in each other's arms and listened to the ocean sing, and the winds wave to us from afar.

This is, of course, when we made Lily.

As if somehow it had all been part of a plan, we dressed matter-of-factly without words and were soon sitting together. My arm was around Ly, and her head was perfectly snug inside my neck. For a long time, we simply sat there and stared at the waterfall and the ocean beyond without saying a word. All we could hear was the constant hum of the water falling with the more distant back and forth of the ocean swell. Likely because we were so cocooned in nature at that moment, all I could think about was how happy I was and that I wasn't sure for how long I had been smiling. It was probably because we were so close to nature, but I suddenly thought about the seasons and life. The snow that had capped the mountains months before, only to melt through spring to turn into the waterfall that framed our view before us. I thought of the person who had put up the ENTRY FORBIDDEN sign and thought of a "Do not disturb" sign on a hotel room. In its own way, the man-made part, the sign, had been perfect too.

I realized Ly was no longer in my arms and was handing me a plate of sandwiches and filling a cup of tea from a flask in front of me. I took one long look at her. Her hair by her shoulders, which I had never seen before, her eyes that sparkled like the waterfall, her face natural without makeup and her jeans and white shirt look, which was so novel to see her in after all these months of formality. And well, I was frankly enchanted.

I thought about my journey to this spot and this time. I thought of leaving Korea for California, I thought of meeting my Uncle at the airport, I thought of the mechanics boiler suit he proudly presented me with, I thought of the black suit he had me fitted for in San Francisco. I thought of his nervousness when he drove me to meet with Takeshi for the first time in Pebble Beach. I remembered meeting Takeshi for the first time. A ten-minute meeting may be less. Perfunctory, he asked how good my Japanese was. "Good enough, but not too good. I don't want you listening to more than my basic instructions. You may hear conversations from the back of the car that are never to be remembered, even if you do follow the lingo". I remembered driving the Mercedes 600 for the first time. Most of all, I remembered seeing Ly for the first time. I remembered his words; "please take care of my wife".

"Please take care of my wife;" his words lingered with me.

As if anticipating a change of mood, the weather changed just like that. At first, we thought it was the wind blowing the mist from the waterfall our way before we realized it was beginning to rain. It began as a soft, conciliatory rain, a somehow understanding rain that encouraged us to pack up and head back to the car. The path back up seemed to be a lot steeper than the way down, and I noticed the netting on the bank side holding up the slope, which was presumably the reason the area was out of bounds. I took one last look at the scene and froze it into my memory forever.

As I fired up the car, the rain picked up its rhythm and soon became torrential. Suddenly, the weather had a primal feel to it. It forced us to drive back to Pebble Beach in complete silence as I concentrated on the road. Ly was obviously nervous as the rain completely obscured our view of the road in front of us, and all she said was to "concentrate and slow down, please." At that moment, our honeymoon, if we had one, was over so prematurely. The change of weather seemed to force both of us to maybe overthink what lay ahead in more ways than one.

We were processing what had just happened. We both realized that we had done something that would change our lives forever.

Eventually, I pulled the car outside of the house, and the rain had dissipated a little. I could see the housekeeper already waiting by the main door, like a mother hen. I suddenly began to get a grip on reality, and a deep-seated fear began to envelop me; "I had just made love to Takeshi's wife". What spirit on earth had got hold of me?

I didn't have to say it, as she did, "You know, eventually Takeshi will return, and what then?". She began to sob, and the tears ran down her face that mimicked the raindrops on the windscreen of the Porsche. They were slow and determined.

I tried to reach out to her, but she pushed me away, gently but purposefully.

She looked at me coldly for the first time and turned her back to me as she opened the car door and walked to the house, leaving me frozen by the car, both of us resigned to our fate. I don't know why, but this wasn't like the movies. I didn't follow her, the old Bonsai that existed before that day was returning. I simply wasn't mature or experienced enough to know what to do. I was a simple young mechanic, after all.

Bonsai

Thirty years have passed since that day, and here I was at the Shed where of course, I returned that Porsche and I don't suppose it was ever driven since. The security man looked at me nervously and was somewhat satisfied that my details checked out. He looked like the kind of man who never watched television and lived for his job as a caretaker, in the darkness of the Shed with all these beautiful items, like a zookeeper. The perfect man for this job, as he likely never recognized anyone, let alone anyone famous, providing the other patrons with the anonymity they demanded when they came to play with their toys.

After checking out my ID, the security guard ushered me into the back of a golf cart and drove me around to Takeshi's shed. It felt like I was being driven around some sort of film studio and being taken to the prop shed.

When we got to Hanger 6, the security man entered some numbers, and in short order, the door was open, and the light was on. The hanger was at once lit up, and the contents of the treasure box were revealed. A lifetime of collecting cars stood in front of me. Cars which Takeshi, for the most part, had never seen in the so-called flesh, let alone driven. I wondered if the security man was the same person who took care of all the cars. The room was full of some of the most collectable cars on the planet. My eyes, of course, were drawn to only one thing, the emerald green 1978 Porsche 911

Sandy Nicolson

T. Just like the emerald water that flowed from the waterfall that day. Undoubtedly, at any level, the car had been frozen here in time almost ever since. A real museum piece to our lives.

To wake me from my daydream, the security man was giving me the keys to the Mercedes 600, which was already parked in front of the entrance door.

"My instructions are to give you these, and this is the car you are to drive until its return, whenever that may be".

"Nice to see you again," I said.

"Sorry, what did you say?" said the security guard.

"I was talking to the car. It's a long story:" and he didn't have to answer, he didn't reply.

In a beat, I was in the driver's seat and back out on the highway. I was relieved to be out of there and be able to breathe again. Seeing the Porsche was like seeing a ghost. I made my way towards the Airport and braced myself for whatever was going to happen next.

Chapter 12

After Pfeiffer Falls, Bonsai has to hustle

As you have worked out by now, well my life has never been the same since that day at the waterfall.

The next day was the start of that new chapter. As usual, I arrived in the Limo to pick up Ly. It may seem strange, but I could sense something was wrong. From the moment my Uncle and I couldn't get a truck disengaged early that morning at "fill up", the world seemed out of kilter, and I was stuck to a behemoth now whether I liked it or not. Like the gas pump, we couldn't disengage from the truck. I, too, was stuck. It felt like the world wasn't flowing in harmony anymore.

When I went to pick up Ly, she arrived at the top of the steps at the Pebble Beach house in her "old clothes"; a silk; "Takeshi" dress, her hair in a bun and her makeup perfectly done. Again, she looked like his Geisha girl. I opened the door for her and said good morning and tried to smile with my eyes. As the housekeeper looked on, she gave nothing in return.

When we got in the car, she broke my heart and said, "I don't want to talk. I just want to think." The mercuriality I had seen in her eyes the first time I met her and attracted me to her was now coming back to haunt me.

Sandy Nicolson

After we were out of the driveway, I said, "How are you? Yesterday was the best day of my life," or something along those lines; she looked at me coldly and said, "Yesterday was a mistake:" and after a beat, she added cruelly; "you should be wearing your hat:" she said referring to my driver's hat. I looked at it, sitting in the passenger seat and reluctantly put it on. I was suddenly a servant again.

When we got to Lovers Point, she declined to get out of the car for the first time, saying she just wanted to watch the Ocean in silence. And so, we sat there for hours as the scene changed and slowly began to fill with pedestrians, tourists and local couples. All the time, she was looking West towards Japan and, of course, towards Takeshi. Who, like a great white shark that enjoyed the cold waters of the Pacific, was, of course, out there somewhere and would ultimately decide our fate.

Something in her behavior made me too stubborn or awkward to confront it, in a way, I simply didn't know what to make of it. My mind raced. Did I go mad? Did the waterfall moment really happen? Did someone possess her? Did Takeshi get to her and threaten her already? If so, why had he not confronted me? Was this going to continue forever? What was she expecting me to do? Where had the confidence I had that day gone? Why had she retreated like this? Why did this make me feel like a worthless gas station worker

Bonsai

again in the blink of an eye?

And so, this existence went on for months until, one day, I simply couldn't take it anymore. When we got to our usual car spot. I waited an hour or so, and then I insisted we walk to Lovers Point. Despite pleading previously, this time, she simply nodded. I chaperoned her from the car, and we walked Southwards past the ice plants that had enchanted us just a few months ago, which were now no longer in full bloom. The magical carpet of pink had gone.

We both looked out at the Ocean, which roared in front of us. A world that neither of us understood stood in front of us. I had rehearsed my speech, of course, many times, but now, when it came to it, I couldn't think of any of the words, not one. I began to cry like a child. Full streams of tears ran down my face, and I sobbed uncontrollably. She just stood there, stoical and wore the same solemn face she had worn for months. A poker face that she passed on to me in those days together. It became my mask, too. Eventually, when I had exhausted my tears, she spoke matter of factly, "I am pregnant. I need your help to have the child but Takeshi must never know. Otherwise, he will kill all of us. Whatever you do, do not touch me. They may be watching us. I am assuming Takeshi does not know about my pregnancy, but I cannot be sure. Nod if you understand".

And I did, despite all my desire to bring her into my arms.

Instead, I actually took a step back, blown back by the magnitude of what she had just said. My head was fried. Clearly, part of me was ecstatic. I was going to be a dad. She wanted to have a baby. My baby. But what did she mean, "hide it?" clearly, that seemed like an impossible proposition standing there. It sounded like something from a fable or at least a story from a long time ago, a time truly in the past. I was a mere mechanic, with no one else in my life really aside from my sick Uncle, very few acquaintances, much less anyone I could trust. This whole discussion was sending my head into a tailspin. I needed a whiskey to straighten out. At that point, I didn't really have time to even think about what she meant by; "they are watching us?" Who on earth were "they," and if they were Takeshi associates, surely we were doomed anyway.

I looked at Ly differently, then, I still loved her, of course, but I realized I was in over my head, and she was way more complicated than I was. That demure look in the back of the limo, had it tricked me? I didn't want to think then, or ever for that matter, that that was true, no matter how compelling any facts were.

"I need your help. I want to have the child, but I am going to need you to make arrangements. Can you do that for us?" she was repeating with some intensity.

"Of course," I said, "anything". I felt a deep well of sadness inside well up as she made her metallic instructions and tried as best

I could to conceal it. The tears had now dried from my face with the Pacific wind blowing straight down from the Arctic. She went further with her dagger;

"Takeshi must never know about this. Never. You understand? I am doing this to protect you and our baby, who will be beautiful. It may mean that we will have to make the greatest of sacrifices for our love."

I nodded as I tried to comprehend the magnitude of what she was really asking of me.

"You don't know who Takeshi is. You don't really know. He is a very dangerous man. I have seen it".

I sighed, and for the first time, she smiled back when I replied, "I have no idea what to process here. First of all it seems to me no matter what lies in front of us, we should at least have a second of joy!"

"We will work out a plan. Please, be calm, and we will take care of things," I said.

In truth, I may as well be driving his Porsche again at that moment, as I had no idea what I was saying or what was happening. But it certainly seemed to lighten her mood.

As we walked back to the car, she had to take a step off the path to vomit on the roots of a Cypress tree.

When we got to the car, she said, "You don't need to wear your hat!" and then, by explanation, "You are going to be the father of our child."

And we both smiled but I know that is around the time, as I say, I really began to hone the poker face. Don't get me wrong, fatherhood, when I look back, being Lily's father has been still one of the best things that happened to me. I know everyone has difficult experiences that come with pregnancy and having a child, but I am sure you will agree ours was certainly in the extreme category of tricky.

That night, I am not ashamed to say that I got drunk. I have never been much of a drinking person, but when I got back to Salinas. I went straight to a Saloon on Main Street.

It was a locals' dive bar. It was the kind of bar where, when you walk in for the first few minutes, all the eyes of patrons train to you, like racoon eyes in the dark looking up from a drain. At first, in the half-light, they thought I might be a tourist. If you were as much as you had business, a few dollars to spend, you most likely got a brisk reception. This was squarely a bar for locals to go and get drunk and forget about their toil and, at the same time, give their hard-earned cash back to the beer bank. At first, for sure, they thought I was a tourist until soon enough, the barman and a few

Bonsai

others realized it was me, Bonsai, the somewhat peculiar gas station guy.

"Heavy day at the garage?" the barman said with some sarcasm as he poured me a whiskey and then added, "Didn't recognize you at first in the suit. Who died?"

I simply smiled. I had the luxury of not having to talk much, as, like most of the locals, they presumed my English was limited.

My mind was racing, I was going to be a father to the most beautiful woman in the world, but somehow, we were going to have to have the child in secret. This was 1979, not the fifth century and I was no King that had an illegitimate child with means to hide it. If anyone in my life was that person, that was Takeshi.

So, how on earth were we going to do that? How on earth was I going to do that? And then, what life were we introducing this child to? Did it mean a life on the run? The chances of us outrunning a man like Takeshi with his power and reach were incredibly slim. Then there was death. It was almost guaranteed if he found out, which he surely would, that he would kill me and the Yakuza we're known for killing people in the most gruesome of ways, but never mind me. What of Ly? She would most certainly be the first to go. The whole thing was hopeless. I didn't know whether to be happy or sad or terrified or all three, so I drank my whiskey and tried to think of an escape. As much as I drank, the whole thing seemed desperate, and the more sober I got.

As the evening went on, I noticed a group of Latino men move through the bar and into the kitchen, which my bar stool happened to have a good view of. In time, I realized that the visitors were here for cards and the players were gathering in the kitchen. I asked the barman if I could play. He shook his head; "Buddy, you need 5k buy-in, you have that kind of cash?"

I don't know what came over me. Maybe it was because, otherwise, I had no other options, but I decided it was my only path. There was no way I would be able to help Ly have our baby and hide it in the legitimate world. So, this was the only chance I would likely have to break into the other world and just maybe find a window of opportunity.

So, I returned to the garage and took $5k from my Uncle's life savings while he was sleeping. I am not proud of it, but without it well, Lily wouldn't have had a chance. Not that it's an excuse, but he was dying, of course. All I had to lose, well, everything really you could ever have. Ironically, this was a moment where, much later, I would reflect that it was also an important day, as it was really the day I fell into the underground poker world in a very different way. Bounce games here and there, that characterized my love of poker up and to the point. I traded in for something that became a lifelong habit.

Bonsai

When I returned to the bar, the barman had already told the crew that the "Chink" garage guy, who was knee-deep already in liquor, wanted to join the game, and apparently, he had the funds. The Artisan had said it was okay, and so it was okay; "I am sick of playing with the same people anyway," he had said. But in reality, they likely thought it was easy; "pick up" money.

Rodriguez, or "The Artisan" as he was known, ran all of the illegitimate pursuits in Salinas and, by now, most of the legitimate enterprises, too. In the real world, he was really an American dream story, a Mexican immigrant who ran one of the largest agricultural businesses in the Salinas Valley. On one level, an upstanding citizen, an employer of hundreds of people, an active member of the non-profit scene, a sometime councilor, and a taxpayer. But of course, he had another side, a racketeer, a gambler, an enforcer, a debt collector, a murderer. If you read the local newspaper and read the dispatches, that is the character Rodriguez would be very happy you saw. But whilst he appeared in good light any given week, pages 1 - 20 say, well, let's just say a number of the obituaries at the end of the paper belonged to him too.

He actually did look like; a "so-called" upstanding citizen. If you were casting him in a part for a movie and you wanted someone to be, let's say, the father of the bride in a romantic comedy or the virtuous prosecutor in a detective series, Rodriquez was your man.

Sandy Nicolson

He was a tall man with noble chiseled features, meticulously groomed slicked back black hair and, a powerful gait that had immediate presence when he entered a room and let's not forget, a perfectly trimmed mustache. In the Valley, he was a very powerful man.

Poker, for all the skill it requires, whether you win or lose over time, is ultimately defined by luck. In my early years In Salinas, I have had luck and lost it in equal measure.

In my life, too, I have had luck to emigrate, luck to get a job working with my Uncle, luck to drive for Takeshi, luck to meet Ly…….luck to have a child, of course. Although, that part I wasn't 100 percent convinced of that particular night.

It wasn't by design, but I simply hadn't changed from driving Ly that day, and so, sort of accidentally, I looked the part for the game, in my black suit and white shirt. When I returned to the saloon, I was ushered into the kitchen. One of Rodriguez's men frisked me and then asked for my proof of buy-in. I cautiously gave him half of the cash I had taken from my Uncle.

When I got to the table and ordered a whiskey from the same guy that had been serving me at the bar earlier in the evening; they asked for my name. "Not your real name, but a name for when you play with us?".

"If you don't have one, sure, we'll give you one," one of them sniggered.

I searched my mind and then I remembered Ly and I earlier in the summer, sitting together looking at those Cyprus Trees in Pebble Beach.

"It looks like a massive Bonsai tree, don't you think?" Ly had said.

So, Bonsai it is.

I managed to play respectfully and ended up splitting the winnings with the Artisan. In the end, I was up on the night, surprisingly to his men, with two thousand cold ones. It wasn't by design, but it was conveniently the right thing to do to pay "tax" to the Artisan. And at the end of the game, I seemed to have made a solid impression. Although, naively, I was to realize later that the Artisan's entrepreneurial cogs never stopped turning, and the prospect of cheaper gas would come in handy for him and his crew in due course. At any rate, I was invited to join what were known as the "tour" games. The "tour" games were much higher stakes and got their name on account of the players that joined from out of town. In return, playing had given me a short fix, and frankly, a short-term evening fix from the inescapable truth that Ly was pregnant and I was otherwise a dead man, So I really didn't have anything to lose. And somehow, I was clinging to the hope that this underground scene, which I really wasn't made for, may somehow give me a chance of finding a way to bring our child into the world without, at least, all of us getting killed.

The next "tour" game was to take place in the Victorian Inn in Salinas. These games weren't played in the shabby kitchen of a dead-end saloon. So, in this case, my first game, the invite was to an Inn that had been there for hundreds of years and had equally seen hundreds of card games from countless journeymen and cowboys passing through town.

The one thing with winning at poker in the underground scene that is particularly unusual given the "day jobs" some of the players have (let's just say that they aren't all 9-5 ers) is that there is a lot more respect than you think if you win. Bizarrely, and this is something I have learned over the years, is that unless you insult someone, you can actually walk with your winnings. In fact, you might even say it is fairer than a Vegas casino in the so-called legitimate world. However, the other unsaid rule is that once you are in the club, Hotel California style, there is no escape until you run out of money, that is, enough to compete. Until that day you must come back, you must come back and play. That is an indisputable rule. If you leave and don't return, then, in that case, you are toast.

The night of the game, I wore my suit and my Crockett and Jones. I was somewhat nervous, especially as my English was still a little shaky. I knew how to say "card" and how to bet, so I figured, though, I had all I needed.

I was told at reception to ask for a key to room 15, which I did.

I was soon ushered through the small restaurant. There weren't many patrons. An elderly couple and what looked like a middle-aged traveling salesman on his own.

We then cut through the small kitchen that looked like it had a staff of one.

Soon, we were out back and walking towards an outhouse lit up at the rear of the hotel. There was a burly guy on the door, presumably a guard of some kind. My guide opened the door and left me by simply saying, "good luck". I felt the five thousand dollar stack of notes in my chest pocket for the first time since I pulled up at the spooky-looking place.

Inside the hut was a buzz of energy. There were six seats at the table. Four were occupied, and two men stood by a bar of sorts, speaking conspiratorially, a bottle of whiskey and two glasses between them. At first, no one acknowledged me. Eventually, a tall, smart-looking man with a mustache stood up and smiled. It was Rodriguez.

"Welcome," he boomed, and when he spoke, everyone else

in the room stopped and turned in my direction. With the exception of Rodriguez, they all looked at me suspiciously.

"Come, Gentlemen, we must make our guest feel at home," Rodriguez spoke with authority, and before I knew it, he had stepped round from his seat at the card table and had his hand on my shoulder.

"You are quite the card player, Bonsai. I have seen it. We love to have new talent join our table, don't we, Gentleman;" he said rhetorically and then proceeded to introduce me to each of the players;

"So, this is Constantis. Forgive us for our nicknames, but we call him the "Greek."

Constantis was a wiry man that looked like he would blow over with the slightest breeze. I doubted he ate. He had a nervous disposition, and as I got to know him, I would give up trying to get him to look me in the eye. He looked at me very briefly and nervously and then just as quickly looked away.

"This is the Cook. It's been so long I have forgotten his real name." This time, the face was a welcoming one, deceptively so. It belonged to Luca, of Italian descent but second generation Salinas. His family owned two restaurants in town, which I would learn were the best. He was smoking the largest cigar I have ever seen, and he

Bonsai

immediately extended a fat hand towards me, which I shook. Then, finally, Tucker and Fitz, who I think you may have met before. They were both working men who had graduated from the fields to be bosses. Hard men with skin that had been baked in the sun and had been stretched like leather. They both had eyes that had long since been drained of any emotion, with no doubt about the things they had seen.

"We know the chink;" Tucker said with a sinister smile, and Fitz chuckled, but the joke escaped me.

There was a lady too in the room that wasn't introduced but it became apparent that she was the staff. She shortly took my order, a whiskey and water, which was in front of me as soon as I could blink.

A beat wasn't missed before the cards were being assembled and cut. Tucker assumed the role of banker and asked me to make the cut.

I pulled part of my stash, a $1,000 bundle, from my pocket and exchanged it for chips.

I lit a cigarette to steady my nerves. The room was already thick from smoke from the Cook's cigar, and it hung in the air like an evening fog over a redwood forest in the Big Sur.

Soon, the cards were being dealt. I looked at my watch, and

Sandy Nicolson

it was just gone past midnight.

I started really badly. I had really bad cards. I had fun bluffing with nothing more than a high card in the third or fourth round and got back $3,000 when I was otherwise down to my last five hundred and debating whether to cash some for some more chips. I was already on my fourth whiskey by then. Enthused by that, I felt like I was beginning to feel a turn with the cards. Everyone folded but for me and Rodriquez. I had two kings and nothing else. He called me and went all in for $5,000. I was sure he was bluffing.

I puffed on my cigarette. The room had taken on a golden brown sepia color like in old photographs of the Midwest. I had nothing to lose, really. To make it more theatrical, the room was covered in pictures of the Midwest. Pictures of Salinas in frontier times and one that caught my eye, of a cowboy lassoing a native American outside a tee-pee. This was 1979. Who knows if that picture is still hanging in that room today? I hope not.

I followed Rodriguez and went all in. I moved my chips slowly into the center of the table.

"Bold," said the Cook.

"I knew he was worth the invite," guffawed Tucker.

Rodriguez's eyes smiled, intimating he was having a good time. I took a sip of my whiskey and waited. It took an age for

Bonsai

Tucker to reveal the last card in the river. There wasn't a sound in the cabin but the click of the clock on the wall.

It was a King. My card was a King.

As he revealed the card. I noticed the expressions of my playing partners had suddenly changed, and not just because of the sight of the King.

I felt something cold and metallic pressed to my head. By the look of the table, all I could think was these new entrants to the room were some kind of rivals for this group. It was rivals, you know, maybe a rival gang? I had no idea, but I did know not to move. All I could do was curse myself. I was, for sure, out of my depth. I didn't move a muscle. The next thing I could see, there were three men in bandanas circling the table. So, that meant four if, but for my friend with the pistol, there was no one else behind me.

"Why do you wear those ridiculous bandanas?" Rodriguez snarled, "I know who you are?"

One of the men pushed his gun down on Rodriguez's hand, revealing two pairs of 8's and 6's.

"Ha' Rodriguez, he (referring to me) would have won. It's not your lucky night, it seems!"

The guy speaking appeared to be the leader. He reprimanded

one of his team, who took a drink of whiskey from the bottle on the table, really like he thought he was one of the cowboys from the Wild West depicted on the wall.

"The money, senor! Your wallets and watches, gentlemen."

"I have no watch," I said, but they paid me no interest. Instead, they took the purse from Tucker, and one of them dumped the pile of cash on the table into a black velvet bag that looked like a magicians'.

I didn't move a muscle and prayed to keep my seeming anonymity and the remaining cash in my chest pocket. I was even for the night if I kept it.

Suddenly, there were the sounds of police sirens outside, far off but getting closer. That spurred these cowboys into a sense of urgency, and as fast as they had entered the room, they were gone.

Somebody suddenly yanked at my shoulder and whispered loudly in my ear to "run". The lights in the room went out. I pivoted from the chair and followed a shadow in front of me as they made it out through French doors to the rear of the room and. I just ran as fast as I could after them and into the black ink that was the forest at the rear of the hotel. Powered by adrenaline, I fought my way through the bush until I got to a lane of sorts and then just kept running. After a mile or so, I realized that no one was around and the shadow I had originally followed had long since disappeared, and there was no one behind me. Not a soul.

In a weird way, it was an anti-climax. I lit a cigarette and gathered my thoughts. I really needed to go back and get my car, I decided. Bizarrely, when I got back the place was empty. There were no police cars, or any other cars for that matter, apart from my one. I looked around, and the only thing that was keeping me company were the stars. So, I drove back to the garage in silence and went to bed.

I never found out what really went on that night. But I am pretty convinced it might have been some sort of strange initiation ceremony. Would I fold under pressure? Would I involve myself in gang politics? Would I go to the police? Would I balk at the $5k buy-in? Would my face fit? Would I panic and pull a gun in a distressed situation? Well, if that is what it was, then I obviously passed the test. Following that night, I was invited every Saturday to the regular Saloon game, and of course, I turned up and lost and won like clockwork, to begin with, that is. Bonsai had a seat at the table then.

In the months that followed, my life sunk into a strange limbo. I don't remember sleeping much. Maybe I didn't. Aside from a tourist pamphlet of Pfeiffer Falls that I kept in my pocket, at all times, it was otherwise like that particular day never existed.

Sandy Nicolson

At 4:30am, I opened the garage. In those days, my Uncle was getting sicker and sicker and rarely rose from his bedroom early. On the rare days he did, he would sit on a bench out front and watch the sunrise, convinced it would be his last. Fortunately, he was just about well enough to man the front desk when, at 6:45 am, I drove to pick up Ly. In those days, there were no hand-in-hand walks anymore, and with each day, we seemed to grow apart. In retrospect, I think she withdrew deliberately, somehow, thinking I would be hurt less when the inevitable parting happened.

She would insist on sitting in the back seat of the limo and just watch through the tinted windows with melancholy as the Lovers Point scene changed as the rest of the world woke up and gradually filled it with some activity. All the time, I would sit up front and stare at her belly through her "Takeshi" silk dresses.

If you didn't know, even until deep into her third trimester, you would never know she was pregnant. It made me smile ironically. You would never know I was the father either, for that matter. From what she knew, if Takeshi got the release date he was going to get, she would give birth just before. If she served the full term. She would share these types of facts solemnly from the back of the limo. As we got closer to the due date, she told me about her fate I had begun to resign myself that she would need to go to Japan to be with Takeshi on his release.

Chapter 13
How Did Bonsai Hide Moses?

I needed to make arrangements so that the baby could never be traced by Takeshi. I told Ly I was working on a plan. But in truth, both of us didn't really have a clue at that point what was going to happen next.

I would spend the evenings playing poker and drinking whiskey in the town. The guys I played with were the underbelly of Salinas, the crooks, the thieves, the cheats, the muscles, the bad guys. But for some reason, they never asked me to join them on any of their enterprises. Sure, when they came to my gas station, I never charged them, but that wasn't a crime.

I never thought about it, but it was the same with these folks as with Takeshi. I always waited in the car, so to speak, I never saw what went on inside, and I never asked. I never tried to work out what they were doing, as Takeshi had instructed me when I first started driving with him. Keep your Japanese basic and your eyes on the road, he had told me. You are my driver, that's it, he had said. So, was the parallel with these folks? I didn't know and didn't care what went on in the so-called "other room." I kept my eyes on the cards. I am sure I was morally ambivalent. I was just not a hero. And besides, as you know I had enough problems to deal with to get involved in more trouble.

Sandy Nicolson

In a strange way, when I reflected on it in those evenings, drinking whiskey and playing poker, Takeshi had treated me like a son in a way. He had protected or shielded me from whatever he was involved in. I had heard the rumors, of course. Ly herself had called him a; "very dangerous man," but I had never seen it firsthand. I had no appetite for violence anyway. Maybe that is what attracted Ly to me compared to the men she had been surrounded with.

Years later, when my daughter would pound my chest, all I could do was look at her vacantly. "Are you finished?" I would say. And so, it was the same with the Salinas men. They just saw me as the poker guy. In some ways, I was maybe a reassuring presence for them. Stoically sitting there night after night playing poker and drinking whiskey and causing no harm. In some ways, it was essential for them that I didn't know and had seen what they saw. In a strange way, I was their security blanket. When they got to the table to escape their own struggles, "Hey, Bonsai". I was like a warm, dependable whiskey at the end of the day. I had only oil but no blood on my hands.

In the final month of her pregnancy, as if on cue, my Uncle passed away. I found him slumped on the bench out front when I returned from Pacific Grove one morning. He had seen his last sunset. I felt guilty in some ways. In the previous months, I had been completely absent, driving Ly and playing cards. More than that, with his failing health, maybe I should have been there more to help

Bonsai

with the garage. He had been good to me, and I loved him. But in a weird way, he died the way he wanted to, outside his garage in the sun in Salinas, his mouth asking the earth one final question.

I told Ly that I would have to take a break from my drives for a week so that I could organize his funeral and attend to his affairs. It just so happened that at the same time, she had spoken to Takeshi, and he was to be released from Prison shortly. I must admit I was completely overwhelmed by all of this, with the result that I think this is the period that killed any final emotional sinew I had left. This is the period that left me with my ultimate poker face.

In a normal relationship, whatever that is, and presuming what Ly and I had was a relationship, having your partner play poker and drink whiskey all night would likely lead to conflict, arguments, ultimatums, and maybe forced into rehab or similar. My circumstance wasn't altogether normal, though, as you have already gathered. It was maybe a function of her pregnancy that we showed solidarity with our mutual and increasing tiredness each morning when we met.

All the teenage boys that passed the Mercedes 600 limo parked in Lovers Point all these mornings with its blackout windows in 1979, imagining what was going on inside, what shady deals were being cut, what celebrity might be there. What movie contracts were being negotiated, business deals executed or something more sinister - which would no doubt color the conversation of the rest of their walk to school. It would likely be beyond their imagination that, in reality, Ly spent the two months before Lily's birth instructing me on what I needed to be ready for to raise a baby potentially on my own.

I didn't realize then, at least not consciously, that Ly knew that when she went to Japan when Takeshi was released, she may not be coming back. I know now that she was getting ready to make the ultimate sacrifice. In other words, leaving her baby, our baby, Lily, with me.

Those were the days of lists. Ly insisted that I buy a notebook and I would sit in the front of the Limo, taking down her instructions methodically. Ironically, I never used the book. In the end, raising Lily was far too chaotic for lists.

As the time grew nearer to her due date (and Takeshi's release), we planned the day like it was a great train robbery. We even did a dry run like we were going to a real hospital. She had never been to the gas station but she wanted to know specifically where my telephone was in the gas station. How far away I would need to be before I would hear it? How long would it take to drive from the gas station to the house in Pebble Beach, and in return, how long would it take to get to the farm?

You see, "The farm;" was to be our general hospital.

I had learnt about the "farm" in one of my poker games and, most importantly, a lady they called "Abuela", the grandmother.

Bonsai

I had actually seen the lady they called; "Abuela" before. She delivered food; homemade chili, salsa and occasionally enchiladas to the boys in the Saloon. It turned out she was a lady with many skills. She was the Artisan's mother and, most importantly, had been a veterinary nurse. Her medical skills were put to good use by the local gangsters, and she had helped avoid many of them going to a regular hospital where there would otherwise be an inconvenient record of their visit. You know, a bullet wound, a stabbing, a broken bone, she could fix you up better than any animal, it seemed.

I was the first person to ask her to deliver a baby, though. Bizarrely, she was excited by the idea. I got the impression that she had lived for so long in an alternate universe, spending her days making chili, fixing bullet and knife wounds at strange hours of the day and delivering farm animals that she had long since lost what regular folks like you might think of as reality. She truly lived and breathed in a secret parallel universe. The fact I had to pay her $5,000 was irrelevant. She was excited at the prospect of bringing her first human baby into the world. Of course, I didn't tell Ly that it would be her first time. The most important thing Ly cared about was whether it could be done in a way that our anonymity could be preserved, and I assured her that would be the case.

Chapter 14

Welcome Lily, Goodbye Ly

On a morning in September 28, 1980, the housekeeper came out to the car and told me that Ly wasn't feeling well, so she wouldn't be driving today. So, I went to Lovers Point on my own. I parked the car and walked out to the rocks. It was a Sunday, and I had closed the garage for the day. With my Uncle's passing, I would need to find another person to cover for me and help in the store, but that was a challenge for another day.

I sat on the rocks and took in where I was physically and mentally. I didn't know then, that was probably one of the last times I had a sense of peace for the following 30 years. When I returned to the garage, the phone was ringing, and as it turned out, it had been ringing nonstop for hours.

It took me a moment to work out it was Ly on the other end of the line, such was her distress, like she had been shot in the gut.

"Where have you been? I don't think I can make it," she screamed.

I drove as fast as I could, ignoring stop signs and the whole world apart from the road in front of me was a complete blur. Of course, I knew the road like the back of my hand, and I was a driver, so that helped to get there in no time flat. I don't think I had ever

Bonsai

asked as much of my old Ford 150, though.

Once I had collected her, I drove to a farmhouse not far from here where a "nurse" was waiting. She hardly made a noise through labor as if internalizing the suffering. That had clearly been something that she had experienced even before childbirth, I realized later. She was in great pain.

I held her hand the whole time, and Abuela worked tirelessly with warm towels and administering painkillers. I had to stop myself thinking of her working as she usually did to help animals to give birth but of course, there is not a huge difference really. All I hoped, of course, was that there were no complications, not least as we hadn't seen any doctor whatsoever throughout the pregnancy. Six hours later, as the sun rose, our beautiful daughter was born. Abuela put her on the baking scales in the kitchen; she weighed 6 pounds flat.

Ly then slept, and I couldn't stop smiling at our beautiful baby. I switched from holding Ly's hand to holding hers. On the wall of the kitchen, behind her crib, was a very simple childlike picture. I do not know if this is true, and I never asked her in her lifetime if it was painted by one of her very own but it was a simple still life of a vase of lilies that had most certainly been painted by a child. And that is how our daughter got her name.

I wasn't thinking straight then, of course. These were

extraordinary times. Ultimately, Abuela told me that I was no help there and should freshen up and let Ly sleep. "Come back tomorrow, please".

I thanked her, of course and took her instruction.

I came back to the gas station, had a shower and freshened up. I think I may even have had a small whiskey and then slept the longest and deepest sleep of my life. I awoke the next morning and almost wondered if the whole thing was real. At that point, every single part of my life felt like a complete work of fiction.

When I returned to the farmhouse. The world I had left had changed. My world had changed.

Lily was in a crib on a table in the center of the kitchen sleeping.

Ly stood immaculately dressed in a designer trouser suit that she must have packed. Her makeup, perfectly painted. She looked completely alien in that farmhouse. But more than that, it was surreal that she had a baby just hours before. You would never have known. She had a look I hadn't seen before, maybe pronounced by her dress and the contrast with having just had a child, but most importantly, her face was stern, business-like.

She spoke to me first in Japanese.

Bonsai

"Take me to the house, please," she said matter of factly, adding, "We must leave the baby here".

I nodded my understanding.

She then walked to the crib, and there were no words. It was as if she was in a trance. She lifted Lilly into her arms gently. Neither Ly or the baby cried.

Ly swaddled her child and stood there, rooted to the spot like an old Cypress tree with a single bird's nest perched up high. The large glass window behind framed her with the fall's pending harvest in the fields beyond. At that moment, she looked like she was showing us a window to a different time and place. The setting sun shone in from the fields, giving them a warm glow. The scene was ephemeral and perfect. It looked like an oil picture from another time.

Then, as if some maternal supernatural telepathic force commanded it, she hugged Abuela without words. They were both stoical people at that moment. At least on the outside. The emotion was internalized. They were like rocks on Lovers Point.

I didn't realize until much later she was saying her deepest thank you to Abuela, and in return, Abuela was saying without words, "I understand, and I will".

Then Ly turned to me and said simply, "Driver, we must go".

Sandy Nicolson

Leaving Lily and driving back to Pebble Beach in my old pick up was the most awful drive of my life. I was so emotional I couldn't speak. Instead, this new Ly had been born, and she did all the talking matter-of-factly, and I wondered later if she had rehearsed her lines. In other words, she knew all along this was going to be how it had to be.

I must admit, and I am sure even in normal circumstances, this is true with the birth of a child, but I was in a state of bewilderment.

For some reason, the fact we were in my own Ford pickup, rather than Takeshi's car for the ride to his home, piqued the feeling of disruption that was in play. This feeling was completely amplified by the contrast between Ly's giving birth 24 hours previously and now in her business-like trouser suit, a type of outfit I have never seen her wear. Her hair pulled back in a matter-of-fact ponytail. Her face resigned to a different destiny. In contrast, I looked like a farmer hick by the wheel of the old Ford pick up truck. We were suddenly and completely in different worlds. It was the most unlikely scene for two new parents.

She didn't want to speak on the journey and much to my chagrin, I respected that. I put it down to tiredness, and at that point, Takeshi could not have been further from my mind, even when we pulled up at his house. Only then did she speak, and these words, I will never forget.

Bonsai

"Please return to our daughter and be the father you need to be. I love you for everything. Sometimes, fate has a power that we do not understand. I have complete faith that you will do the right thing".

She then kissed me. A kiss that said she was doing everything to contain her emotions, and she was asking me not to break the seal.

"You are amazing, and I simply love you," I said in return.

She stepped out of the truck. The housekeeper was waiting at the top step. I took her bag from the back of the pickup and handed it to her.

"You will call me when you want me to collect you?" I added.

She looked at me with a poker face and then turned and walked up the front steps of the house. The housekeeper closed the door, and she was gone. Just as she disappeared behind the door, I realized afterward her back had sagged slightly as she crossed the threshold.

I returned to see Abeula and Lily and sat with them until midnight. Marveling at our new miracle and Abeula's efficiency at giving Lily milk, she had presumably taken it from Ly. For an old lady, she had incredible stamina, which I suppose comes with working off the land for all her life.

I was exhausted emotionally, mostly. I wanted to respect Ly's need to rest but couldn't stand not seeing her. So, I was conflicted when I left Lily to go to the gas station to wait by the phone all night. When it didn't ring after sunrise, I drove back to Takeshi's house. There wasn't a soul on the 17-mile drive, and I felt like the mansions I passed were looking at me expectantly somehow, like giant Greek rock gods. I was obviously exhausted.

To my horror, when I got to the front gate, rather than open as it usually would, to the sweeping arc of a driveway, it was shut and locked. The house was uncannily without any light whatsoever. I scaled the gate and staked out the huge mansion. I suddenly had a terrible, irrational fear. I ran to the front door and banged on with all my might. I screamed, "Ly, it's me!!!" I banged until my legs gave way, and I slumped to the floor. At this point, a hall light illuminated the glass surrounding the door. With a scramble of locks being undone, eventually the door opened, and I looked up and it was the housekeeper looking down at me with a trace of pity.

I looked up at her like she was some perverse reverse of the Statue of Liberty. She looked down at me and simply said,

"I am afraid she had to leave unexpectedly to travel to Japan. You see, her husband, Takeshi-San, was released today".

Chapter 15

The Source Of Lauren's Pain

I let Lily indulge herself with the belief that she had the most suffering as a child. Sure, she escaped a bunch of trauma and, through her grit and hard work, achieved this illustrious career as a lawyer and, of course, became my girlfriend.

She never asked, never really asked about my upbringing. From the moment I told her the lie that I was an interior designer, ah ha, it all made sense to her. The cliche was perfect. When she scolded me for having an extra glass of wine, she didn't realize it was to numb the pain. Not just the pain of seeing the dysfunctionality of life play out every day on the streets of San Francisco but the discord I had seen first hand as a child.

You see, I decided I wanted to be a cop when I was 14.

I was in my freshman year. Of course, I went to an affluent private school in Menlo Park. The kind of school that technically had a waitlist, but in reality, if you were on it, you would be waiting forever. My father's money came from old money, not the new tech kind. My Great Grandfather founded one of the original Savings Banks in the Bay. It sounded very noble, but he was an original loan shark, lending money to GIs returning from the First World War. My father had inherited his ruthlessness, and in place of GIs were presently dot-com entrepreneurs who lost everything in the dot.com crash of the early 2000s. When a financial crisis came and went, my family was kind who were so inherently wealthy we were completely insulated. So, my father was able to lend these tech soldiers in return for equity in their new ventures and then squeeze for return.

Our Lacrosse team had won the Bay Area championships that year, when I was 14 that is. I suppose I was one of the key players. I played attack. It wasn't just goal scoring and my speed I brought to the team, I was aggressive or passionate depending upon which way you looked at it. Or whether you were on my team or in the opposition. For all my doll-like looks, I was tough, and my coach noticed.

Few people knew though, my intensity came from frustration at home. My family always had an apartment in New York. A sprawling apartment in a mansion block on the Upper East Side. In happier times, it was a place we would go to at Christmas. When my grandfather was alive, we would have magical times there. He would dress up as Santa Clause and have all kinds of elaborate ways' he would hide my sister and my presents.

That was all before my mother realized, shortly after my sister was born, that my father was carrying on a double life and his mistress in New York had graduated to become the mother of his child. Bizarrely, the mistress gave birth the day after my sister was born. For some time, my mother had hired a private investigator. She had known he was having an affair, but the fact he didn't show up for my sister's birth but was instead side by side with his mistress in a New York infirmary was the straw that pushed her to file for divorce.

It wasn't about a broken heart, though. Rather, it was the shame that brought my mother into her social circle. The story had broken in the press. It was a minor story of sorts, who cares about a financier having an affair? That happens every other day, of course. However, a New York Times journalist was doing a Clinton-era expose of powerful men who were abusing their positions, and my father's mistress was an intern, so there were parallels to some extent. My mother hadn't really loved my father for some time. In fact, I doubt she ever really did. It was the Peninsula equivalent of an arranged marriage. Her family was even wealthier than my father's and went all the way back to the Gold Rush. They owned vast amounts of real estate in the Bay Area and especially in San Francisco.

When the news broke that he, too, was having an affair and his intern had his baby, the story was immediately put out for discussion on all the news Channels, and my mother just so happened to have been at her Country Club at the time. She was most likely in the middle of one of her self-centered stories when she realized her girlfriends were no longer paying attention; "hey, that's Duke's picture on television!" and; "Turn it up!" someone had said.

The day after we won the Championship, we were scheduled to have our team photograph taken. The photograph was then to have the prestige of being hung in the sports clubhouse. For most of the girls, this was the prospect of being immortalized on the wall alongside the greatest athletes the school had ever produced. It just so happened it was the day, I forgot to bring my uniform to school.

I realized this after morning recess, and my best friend, Emily, pleaded with me to go home and get it.

It was around that time that my mom was more and more absent. It was before she did it, but in retrospect, the signs were there. She would leave my sister with the nanny and disappear for hours. We would discover later that she went to a biker bar near Half Moon Bay, dressed in a leisure suit, and drank her afternoon away. The only thing that was coming on the television behind that bar, wasn't Country Club CNN reports, but say some college basketball game that she couldn't care less about. It was a safe place in that regard, and she was there for the liquor, of course.

I don't know why I did it, but I knew that even if my mother did pick up my call, she would be in no state to drive me, nor did I

Bonsai

want to see her drunk. That was before she died years later in a DUI on the Pacific Course Highway. So, I grudgingly called my dad.

It happened that he was in Palo Alto, finishing a meeting.

"I'll be right there," he said almost too eagerly.

At the end of math, I went to the front office and signed out. I then waited outside the front gates of the school. As I waited, I reflected that I hadn't seen him for nearly a month. Since the divorce, my mother had custody of me and my younger sister, who was now 6 years old. If you were being harsh, my sister represented their last attempt to salvage their marriage.

He ended up marrying the intern. She was only 28. Nearly 25 years his junior. There was something weird that I noticed about girls who fall for men nearly twice their age, they seemed to age prematurely. She was no exception, and she looked closer to 40 than 30. At least, I thought so. She was also one of those women that needed to catch their man early. Like subconsciously, they know they are going to age fast and need to grab hold of their man when they can. At least, financially, she certainly got lucky with my dad.

In the early years, my mother initially refused my father's requests for us to stay with him every other weekend. I am not entirely sure what led her to eventually acquiesce. I summarize it as in-synch with her descent into alcoholism rather than a mellowing of her hatred for him.

But those weekend visits didn't last long. I hated it. I felt more betrayed than my mother. I had been a child when the affair happened, but somehow, I felt like I had missed the clues and signs. Irrationally, I thought somehow, if I had seen the early moments of the affair, I might have been able to change the course of history to stop it from happening somehow. I was my father's favorite, after all. Being with them on those weekends just seemed to heighten my sense of embarrassment. Besides, too, they were so in love that it felt like we were imposing, like the awkward friend that should leave the date. And then there was my half-brother. My father thought it was a good idea to force the kid on me so that somehow it would draw me closer to him or prepare me for being a mother one day.

It wasn't long before his black Mercedes was in front of me at school as I thought of why I hated him. Even at this point, it was a strange feeling when I saw him like this. Part of me wanted to kiss him like the old days, and yet part of me hated what he represented in my life.

"Well, this is a pleasant interruption from a bunch of bullshit meetings:" he greeted me with.

"I couldn't give a shit about the picture, but my friends insist. I get it. I don't know why I called you".

Bonsai

"Well, I'm glad you did, kid," he said. I climbed into that car, and we drove towards our old family home in silence.

The purr of Kenny G and the familiar scent of his aftershave lured me into a sense of comfort until he said:

"How is your mother?"

I felt my anger rising.

"What the fuck do you care?" I said and hated myself for being so obvious.

So, we drove on again in silence.

When we got to the house. My father looked a little sheepish. I realized it was actually years since he had been to the old house. My mother had kept the family home as part of the divorce settlement.

"I am not sure if my key fob will still work," he said almost to himself. He clicked the switch on his key ring. I thought to myself it was interesting that after all these years, he had kept it on his key ring.

The gates opened and revealed the familiar driveway to the main house. He drove slowly like he was driving for the first time.

We parked in front of the house, which was Greek revivalist, with its white stucco and cylindrical columns; it looked like it had been lifted from the French Quarter in New Orleans.

For some reason, I paused before opening the door. We both were in silence, like we were both transporting to a time a long time ago.

The irony was that as we both searched through time, as we pieced through fragments of memories of that driveway, the lawn beside it, the swimming pool and tennis court beyond it, you had to really search for happy memories if that is what each of us were looking for.

As if waving the white flag first, he spoke, "You know this is one of the oldest houses in Atherton. I lived in it for seven years, but I can't say I know it. There is something cold about it to me. It might seem like a strange thing to say, but one of the only things I regret is buying it. I wish your mother and I stayed in our apartment in Pacific Heights. Maybe things would have been different if we had".

Before he could say, "We were happy there once," I had opened the front door and was climbing the stairs to my room. The air in the house had a heavy, damp smell to it, and for some reason, the place suddenly felt like a museum. As I searched through the drawers in my room, I got increasingly frustrated that I couldn't find my uniform. I started pulling out the drawers onto the floor. Chaotically, throwing my clothes wildly across the room. I was throwing a tantrum like I was ten years old, and I didn't care. Soon,

Bonsai

my room looked like it was ransacked. I covered my face in my hands and sobbed.

I went to the bathroom and ran the cold tap and wetted my face with a facecloth. I looked in the mirror and ordered myself to straighten up. On no account was he to see that I had been upset. It was then that I remembered that my top was in the laundry. I fetched it and, with it in my hands, I gathered myself.

Momentarily, I was back in the car with my uniform and headed back to school.

We sat in silence for the rest of the journey.

When we got to the school gates, I got out of the car. As I shut the door, I turned and gave him a look that said, "You let me down."

He turned towards me as if, the whole car journey he had been rehearsing a speech he finally had built up the courage to deliver but hadn't. As he was about to speak, I closed the door. I walked halfway up the lane towards the school before I looked back. When I did so, the car was gone.

I decided the day was spoiled for school. If you ever go to the sporting clubhouse in Palo Alto High and look for the picture of the 1998 Lacrosse Team, you will notice the captain is missing from the picture.

Sandy Nicolson

Chapter 16

Takeshi's Perspective When Ly Returns From Pebble Beach In 1979

In 1979, I made a rare mistake, I realized I had the wrong tax accountant. Unfortunately, it was too late. I was jailed in my native Japan as a result, and so was my accountant for a longer period. However, perhaps my accountant disappeared before he served a day. I can't remember. It was a long time ago now.

A lot of people may think I am a bad man. A Yakuza. I don't like the Western interpretation of that designation as "gangster"; it is simply more complicated than that. And that explanation, I will leave it to you to work out.

Maybe I am a bad man. I think that is a lazy description, too. Life is way more complicated than that. Furthermore, whether I am "bad" or not, I don't think it's you or my place to judge me ultimately. All I can tell you is, from my perspective, all I do know is I have fought to survive. Is that not what humans are supposed to do?

In my case, survival means being in a boat in the Pacific from Japan, first to Hawaii, then to San Francisco as a sick child. Or surviving the oppressive internship on my own, or fighting against racism in San Francisco, or against other gangs, or against corporate

Bonsai

competitors, politicians, etc. You get the picture. You don't win those battles just with kind words. You have to use more than that to maintain your existence. You need to use, in some cases, force and sometimes brutal force. It just so happened I was good at surviving it seems.

But 1979 was, if the whole scheme of my life was to be judged and it will be one day, it was not my favorite year let's just say.

My wife had an affair and bore a child to another man. My honor, in return, was broken. As I said, I spent a year in jail, isolated from her. I instructed her to stay in the US and not return to Japan until I was released. I wanted to make sure she was not embroiled in the same mess. I didn't want my bird to be in the cage with me. Or, more precisely, a cage I didn't control.

Like me, my wife was no saint. A madam in a brothel I owned in Tokyo offered her to me when she arrived on a ship from Vietnam and suggested I may choose her to be exclusive to me. When I met her, I didn't have to answer. My madam was under strict instructions to tell no one of her past. She may have disappeared, too, I can't remember. I am no saint, a Yukuza, in your words, a gangster of sorts who has had to execute tasks that you might balk from. As I say, you can't judge me, and nor will I judge you.

In my life, I have seen both love and hate in people's eyes

and everything in between. When Ly returned from Pebble Beach and I was released from prison, I knew that she was never going to love me. Things were left unsaid, to begin with. I knew she had failed my test. The simple driver had indeed screwed her, and they had fallen in love with each other. I had let the whole thing happen after all. A sort of sadomasochistic thing, you might think, like cutting myself before I went to prison. I needed to feel some pain for my mistake. As I said, I don't make mistakes, and there would have to be pain for it to be atoned. The pain needed to be felt by me and others. It was only fair to rebalance things and teach me to be more careful in the future.

I knew that she feared me. In a strange way, that had been an attraction for her before 1979, that is. My power that is. I had suffered enough from my mistake. I decided when I was released from jail. Consequently, now that pain must dissipate from me and belong to others. That is how the world works. There is a constant trade of love and pain between humans, you may not always see it, but it is happening all around you perpetually. That is life. It just so happens that someone like me is an exchange, if you like, of love and hate.

When Ly returned from Pebble Beach and I was released, it was her turn to suffer for her mistake, and I was to be the agent of ensuring that happened. And so, I made sure she never returned to

Bonsai

the US or, even more importantly, had no contact with her child or the driver. I achieved that simply by telling her there must not be. And, of course, she obeyed and suffered the worst pain imaginable as a consequence. You see, that was the worst form of torture I could inflict on her for failing me.

It was probably sick of me, but I developed a fascination for their daughter. The daughter that could have been mine, I supposed. So, I watched from afar her misery growing up in that god-forsaken gas station.

When it was time for her to go to University, my puppet mastery took an interest. What if this smart kid of theirs were to blossom and have a successful corporate career? What could be more painful than not being able to celebrate her success? Either in her father's case because she hated him or in her mother's case because she was ignorant of it. These people were all my toys, I suppose.

So, of course, I ensured she got a Stanford scholarship and, of course, a traineeship in the finest law firm in San Francisco. It goes without saying that I am the kind of man who has the connections to make these things happen.

None of my decisions are extravagant. Everything I have ever done in my life has been with a purpose. Perhaps for that singular mind, I am feared by some, but it is also the reason, eventually, I grew to love and respect Lily. The more I watched her mature, the more I related to her. The more I knew how much her mother was suffering not to know of the blossoming of her child into a successful adult.

So, when I was diagnosed with cancer, it was like a transition note. I knew there was a gift to the God's, the ones that would rightly judge me, I could make, and in return, it was their gift to me. Consequently, I made the decision that the one powerful thing I could do, maybe my final act, would be to end this period of purgatory I had imposed justly on these people. Like when I was released from prison, it was my turn to be the exchange agent again and release them from their hell, and in turn, they may pass their pain on to someone else. Is that not the true circle of life that I have described to you?

I knew that the invite to the golf tournament was a honey trap. Come on, would you think I wouldn't? I invited my adviser to make an appearance at the gas station and make the offer to the driver. I also made other related arrangements, which we will get to in due course.

I set the proverbial chess board with the right pieces and got ready to play with them. The driver didn't disappoint. I knew he wouldn't refuse to be caddy at the ProAm tournament. I knew he wouldn't. From what I knew of him, and that was a lot, he wouldn't accept the offer because of celebrities playing side by side with some of the greatest golfers. No, he was a modest man. A man who arguably gave his whole life to bringing up the child, and despite all of those sacrifices, she hadn't spoken to him for years. A life foregone, sacrifice for her if you will, and for the love of her mother. I also knew he would be scared of me. After all, all these years, he had never had the courage to come and find Ly or myself, not once in Japan. No, I knew there was only one reason he would accept, he still loved Ly. The prospect of seeing Ly as a result of accepting the invite would be overwhelmingly powerful for him. Of course he would accept, for that reason alone.

It was not lost on me, not for a second, that these once-upon-a-time lovers had not changed in thirty years. They had been held frozen in some cryogenic process. What I mean is rather than their respective bodies being frozen in some facility with the hopes of them being brought back to life one day in a different world, in a life-after-death type scenario, in this case, it was their souls that had been frozen by my actions. In this way, physically, they still ostensibly went about their tasks day to day, but the innermost beings had been frozen 30 years ago. Without each other, they were otherwise robots.

You see, when she returned from that year in Pebble Beach in 1980, at my behest when I was set free from my own prison, somehow our positions on one level were reversed. I became a free man again, whilst she became my prisoner again. This time was different. I realized when she returned, she had fallen in love for perhaps the first time. All I could do was cruelly possess her under fear, not for herself but for the man she loved and her child. As I had predicted, all through these years, she didn't fly from the cage, even when the gate was open. Meanwhile, Bonsai loved Lily eternally and yet never tried to escape because he so feared me. As I say, the symmetry of life is perfect.

So, as I share with you my plan to reunite Ly with her lover, it is not out of sentiment. It is because I can. If you judge me in a poor light, so be it. Politely said, I think for you to do so would be naive if you think that your life, dare I say it, has been easy, devoid of the tough choices I had to make. Sure, some of you may not realize that people have to do these things, by which I mean sacrifice, and both endure and inflict necessary pain. Sometimes, we have no option but to do what we do. The universe depends upon us to act. We are the ying to the yang. And we know, as I have known always and especially when Ly returned in 1980, there is a predestined life, and people like me for good or bad, are agents of that force or whatever you want to call it.

So, it is without passion that as I faced the inevitability of my impending death, it must be me who released Ly back into her lover's arms to reunite them and her daughter. It would be my

Bonsai

decision. It was within my power to release them and no one else's. That great privilege had been entrusted to me.

Their torture was justified. For every action, there must be a reaction. Justice must be served, if you will.

So, to bring you up to date with more recent events, since the driver accepted the golf invitation. One week following that, and two weeks ago today, I sat impassively at the deck of my house on the top of hills in Hiroo outside Tokyo, with my plans complete and ready to be executed.

I was looking suitably hawkish, wearing my wayfarers, a black t-shirt, and a white blazer. Despite all my chemotherapy (I was treated in the finest private hospital in Japan), I still hadn't lost my strength, and, if I may say, I still had the looks of a man twenty years younger and in considerably better health. Yet those looks, my power, and gravitas; all of those qualities had meant nothing to her. She loved a gas station owner in Salinas. I don't expect the world to be fair, and I have always led my life on that basis. I took solace from my resolve to that proposition. My whole life, I had not wavered from it. Not one iota.

I knew when I attended business meetings she had sat in this very spot on this very deck and stared eastward across the Pacific toward San Francisco, no doubt longing for them, her lover and her child and their touch.

Sandy Nicolson

Since 1980, she held her empty belly, wondering if she would ever see her baby again. Tears would stream down her face. She had long since lost the sonar signal on her radar identifying the location of their physical presence.

Over the years, her cries had evolved from the yell of a wounded animal to a shriek to a whimper to an internalized ocean of deep internalized pain. Really the worst kind of pain. People will think of a Yakuza doing terrible things with, say, a Samurai sword, but depriving a mother of her child was far more painful. I knew I had witnessed it.

I could only imagine how much she hated me. But, of course, in my company, she was stoical and she showed me nothing. To do otherwise would be to let me win in her mind. I was the Roman emperor, and she was my Spartan slave, of course.

As I sat on my deck that morning, I was having my usual croissant and handful of fruit. She joined me at my request. I asked her to sit and for my housekeeper to attend the table to pour her tea.

I looked out to the Pacific, and I knew I must execute my plan. I couldn't let her see the slightest of hurt when her eyes showed the slightest of light that had been so absent all of these years when I told her my plan. In this case, the roles were about to reverse again and I must not show any glimpse of weakness, any sign that she may have hurt me with her love for them. I controlled the chess table here, after all.

"It is a beautiful morning. The sun rises in the East and sets in the West," I said.

She narrowed her eyes ever so slightly at my cryptic comment. She was like a cat on the ledge that notices a bush move ever so slightly and narrows her stare, curious to what may be there, hidden previously from view.

"That's true:" she said without emotion. Ever since she returned, she made it her business to become fluent in English. I knew why. I didn't let her give me a rise. I was in control, remember over them. So, instead, I ensured that she had the finest private English teachers in Japan, and now, of course, she spoke without the slightest of a Japanese accent. The Ly I knew, the peasant Vietnamese prostitute, had died a long time ago. I had ensured that.

"I need you to pack for a trip. I have been asked to play in a golf tournament in the US. You will accompany me".

She was in my full focus now. Everything around her was a blur. I couldn't tell you if on the banister behind her was a crow, a magpie, a bulbul, or a Sparrow, I couldn't tell you if an Air Japan plane flew overhead at that precise moment or the blossom fell from my Oak trees, all I could see was her face. As the time froze, I could no longer see her hair. I couldn't tell you what she was wearing then, you know the color of her dress, or the color of her cheeks. I could just see her eyes at that moment. And so she blinked and said,

"Of course. How exciting for you. Where is the tournament?"

I could now see only her dark pupils. They were as deep as a garden well in an abandoned garden then.

I looked back out to the Pacific and the sun eager to rise for the new day. I took a sip of tea that had cooled to the perfect temperature.

"It's in Pebble Beach. And you will come with me, and we will stay in the old house".

I could now see the water in the well, and it glinted ever so slightly.

"Will we have guests?"

"It depends on how well I play:" and then I added mechanically, "My driver is here, and you know I can't miss my appointment."

"Of course," she said.

The well lost its light, and a white starling rose and flew toward the Pacific. I followed it for a moment and then lost it in the rising sun.

Chapter 17

Takeshi's Bird Lands, And His Driver Awaits

It didn't take long to go from the Shed to the airstrip in the Limo.

The airstrip was a car park of fancy jets belonging no doubt to the players, the celebrities, and noteworthy folks who had come to play or watch the tournament. The schedule promised there would be a practice round in the afternoon, a welcome dinner and then the tournament. It looked like Takeshi would miss at least some of that, as he arrived late. I suppose someone like him could care less for that entertainment stuff.

As I waited, I stood outside the car, and played with a Pacific Grove ball marker in my pocket to try and ease my nerves on his impending arrival. But my mind wouldn't stop playing over so many scenarios. So many questions ran through my mind;

Was she still with him?

Were they still a couple?

Sandy Nicolson

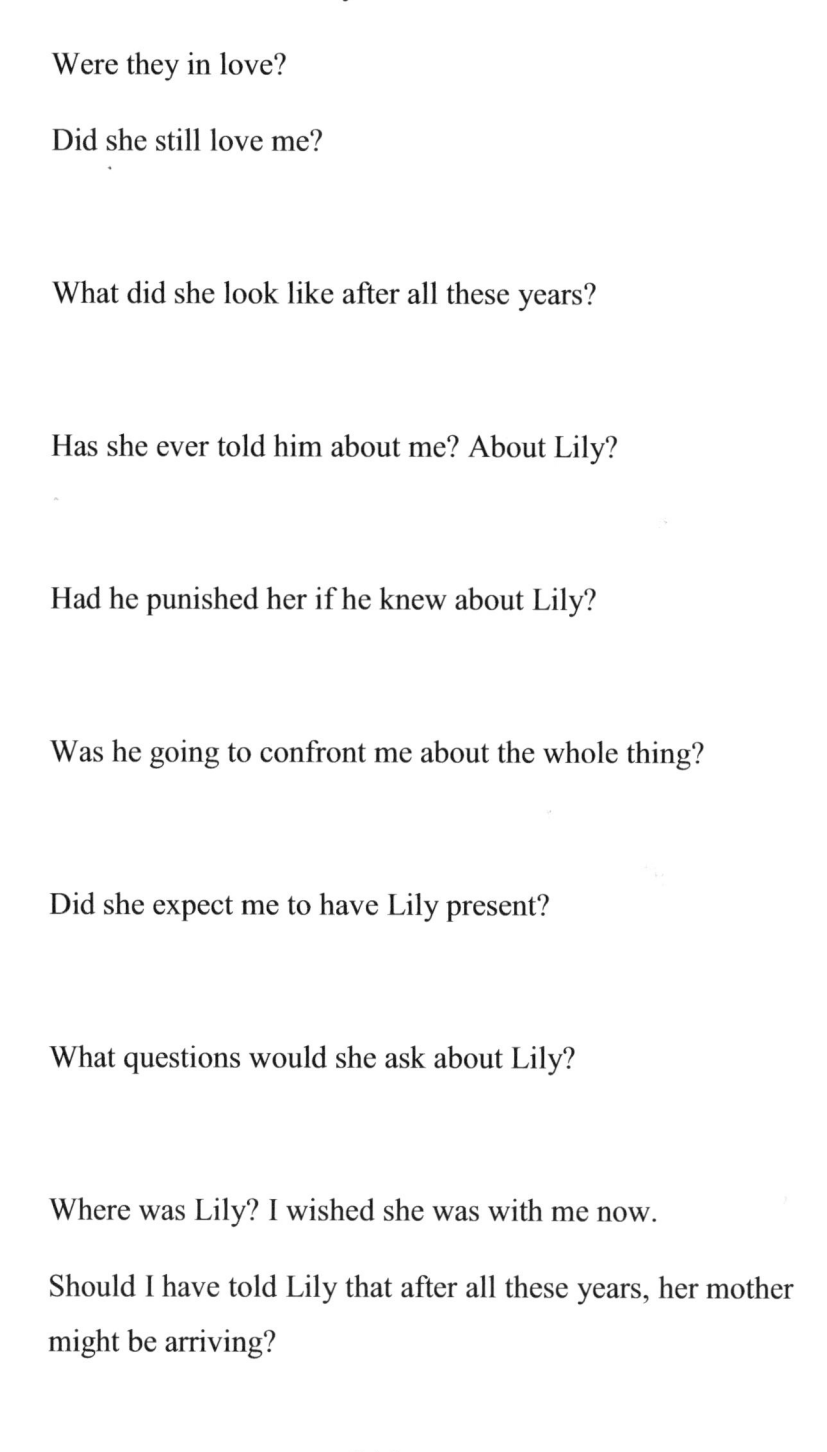

Were they in love?

Did she still love me?

What did she look like after all these years?

Has she ever told him about me? About Lily?

Had he punished her if he knew about Lily?

Was he going to confront me about the whole thing?

Did she expect me to have Lily present?

What questions would she ask about Lily?

Where was Lily? I wished she was with me now.

Should I have told Lily that after all these years, her mother might be arriving?

She might finally meet her mother here, of course. How selfish of me that I had not been thinking about that until now?

Would Lily be disgusted with me that I never had the guts to fly to Japan and try and find her mother?

Should I have tried like a knight in an old story to win her back?

Would she be disgusted that I had never really made anything of my life?

I hadn't moved on a bit since she left. I was the same Bonsai, only more tired and infatuated with someone I had met 30 years ago for a nanosecond. I still didn't even have a 401k pension plan for goodness sake.

And what about my appearance - of course, I had aged - that was to be expected. It had been 30 years, after all. But shucks, I haven't aged well. That California sun, I could blame, I suppose. She was probably still as radiant as ever.

As all of these questions ran through my mind, I could suddenly see a helicopter come into view. It grew closer, and with some kind air of intent. It landed 50 meters from the Limo. Slowly, in time, the blades came to a halt, and the pilot opened the door, climbed out, and walked towards me. I recognized the gait. It was

Sandy Nicolson

Takeshi's adviser who had visited the gas station with the invite all those weeks ago. Soon, he was in front of me and bowed. A man of many talents, it seemed.

"Mister Bonsai, of course," he said by way of an introduction. And before I could reply, he added, as if to reassure me, "Mister Takeshi is on time. You will be pleased to hear."

We stood there in silence like we were two respectful mourners waiting for a casket to enter a funeral scene.

Sure enough, 20 minutes later, a speck on the horizon took the form of Takeshi's gulf stream. As it grew closer, like putting a magnifying glass to a bug, it got larger with inspection. In due course, with a boom of noise, the plane landed. After what seemed like an age, the side door opened, and the landing steps were deployed.

For some reason, I realized I had closed my eyes. I opened them, and there was Takeshi, disembarking on his own. He was wearing a white blazer and black slacks. He had a black t-shirt under his blazer and was wearing Ray Bans. From a distance, he looked pretty much the same as I remembered him from some 30 years ago, but as he got closer to me, I realized that he had unsurprisingly aged considerably. His face looked like a geological map of a National Park. As he grew closer, I couldn't work out whether to focus on him or the plane. I kept watching the cabin

Bonsai

door, hoping she was there and she would soon show herself. But it didn't happen, instead, Takeshi was in front of me, his familiar shark eyes cutting through me. They had not changed one bit. They were azur blue, gleaming and ready to snatch your soul and take it for a spin to the Ocean floor.

"My caddy, I believe. I am very honored that you have agreed to help me this week. Most grateful". And he gave a slight bow, which I returned.

He smiled in a way that made my eyes freeze a little.

Before I could answer, he said, "Now, I don't know if my assistant has told you, but we are going to take a look at the course from above. Plot our path, so to speak, for the round tomorrow. I hope you don't mind helicopters?"

Without waiting for an answer, he ushered me to the helicopter.

"But what about the Limo;" I said.

He smiled in a way that said, never mind about the car, forget about that car.

We buckled up and the Assistant brought the machine to life. The chopper rose from the ground and moved from side to side and in a few seconds, it soared upwards and toward the ocean and Pebble Beach.

Sandy Nicolson

As we looked down over the course, the noise of the blades filled the cabin and prohibited any conversation, which I was thankful for. I just had to try and make sense of what was happening. Much of it was self-imposed, but I had a deep fear of Takeshi. Really, it was all based on hearsay, as I had never actually seen him commit a violent act, but you could tell by his aura he had and had instructed many to do so on his behalf.

If I wanted to, I could have grabbed him and thrown him from the machine, and he could have done the same to me. He was older than me, so you know, I would have the upper hand. And working manually for all these years, of all the things I had lost, I had retained my physical strength.

I wanted to ask him, demand from him what he wanted, where was Ly? What happened to her? But I couldn't because the cabin noise was too loud, and I wasn't sure what exactly I would say after all this time. So, instead, we just sat in relative silence, and I soon realized we were over Pebble Beach and, in fact, continuing to go South. There was a clear blue sky like Takeshi had ordered it. Soon, we were over Bixby Bridge and continued to head South to the Big Sur. A trickle of sweat trickled down my back as I realized we were heading down the same route Ly and I had followed all those years ago in his Porsche 911 T. Sure enough, in no time, we were at Pfeiffer Falls and the "Adviser" expertly landed the chopper

Bonsai

next to the beach. By this point, my heart was thumping, and my blood pressure had risen dramatically.

Takeshi ushered me to get out, and I did. Soon, we were both on the beach, and the chopper, almost as soon as it could, swept away, leaving us both on the beach alone.

Once the burr of the chopper had dissipated into the clouds, Takeshi spoke;

"So, we share the same taste in women, it seems."

I decided in these most dramatic of circumstances, it was best just to listen to him and work out what to do next.

"I told you to take care of her all those years ago, do you remember?"

I suddenly got a sense of my surroundings, the roaring ocean, the echo of the caves, the determined flow of the waterfall, and the inquisitive blue sky. Bizarrely, I felt alive for the first time in thirty years. Whatever was happening, the euphoria of that memory was overwhelming.

I wasn't sure what Takeshi intended, but I figured I really had nothing to lose now. My cards had been dealt.

"I remember," I said. "I fell in love with her." There must be lay lines. I think they call them or something that gives me superpowers on this piece of real estate.

Takeshi didn't answer, instead, he walked toward the surf, and I followed him.

We both stood for a while together, watching the surf break in front of us and the foam run up to just short of our feet, and then as if it were on string, it pulled back out to its own body.

"Why did you never try to reach her? If you loved her, surely you would have climbed the mountain, so to speak. To find her and be with her. Surely you would have wanted to reunite her with her daughter?"

He said, daughter? How did he know? Of course, he knew.

The waterfall sparkled to my left like a mirror ball, making a million suggestions with its perpetual refraction of light.

I steadied my nerves and took a moment to think through his question.

"I actually don't know. I am actually ashamed to say. She painted a terrifying picture of you that is true, and ostensibly, I may have feared for my life if I went in pursuit. That if you found out, you would kill us all in the most grizzly fashion. Absent of that, I took on my responsibility to care for Lily when she was gone. I suppose the whole experience felt so surreal that I didn't deserve to be with someone so beautiful that I had usurped your honor, and so

Bonsai

I kept my head down and took care of the most wonderful gift I had ever been given, being Lily. Days turned into weeks to months to years and time just passed. I got stuck, I suppose, in my melancholy, my only little world. With time, the more distant I got from Ly and your world. The whole thing didn't seem real to me anymore. But there is one more thing. In a funny way, my own honor was hurt when she left the way she did. Of course, as you may, and I don't want to be presumptuous, but if you knew and left me alive, if you accepted it, then well, so did I, at least at some level. Like the ocean that comes and goes as sure as the sun sets and moon rises, it is life".

I took in a big breath of sea air. I had never confessed any of that to anyone, and I suddenly felt a massive amount of relief roar through my body. I didn't care what happened to me now, I had told my truth, and I felt free of a burden I had carried with me for thirty years.

Finally, Takeshi spoke;

"I understand that I may be a very wealthy man, someone with great power, who can have us come here in a helicopter at the drop of a hat. But I will tell you as I watched you, and I have watched you, from afar bringing up Lily, in that god-forsaken gas station, in that town, no matter the wealth I have enjoyed, I have looked on with envy. You have been a great father. I wanted to hate you. I wanted to hate you because Ly has loved you all this time, and frankly she deserved better than someone like you to love her. But I can't hate you. I have let you suffer enough. I have come to tell you

I am letting that go".

We then stood together and looked out to the Ocean and the waves that hopscotched over each other. It was a strange experience but one where you had this feeling not to speak but to let some sort of third force carry you forward.

Eventually, I had to ask the question that had been burning for so long inside me.

"Where is she?"

He looked at me with those shark eyes of his and said frustratingly.

"Not yet".

So for a time, we just stood there, two old men on a beach in Northern California with memories of the same woman, looking out to the horizon.

In due course, the helicopter returned and took us back to Pebble Beach. As I climbed in, relieved in part by the realization that, for now, Takeshi wasn't going to kill me, I smiled, a wide smile I hadn't broken for as long as I could remember, but most importantly, the reason for my levity was, at least the smallest of hopes, but nevertheless hope, that with Ly there may just be more to come.

Chapter 18

Lily takes Lauren to corporate entertainment at the Golf Tournament

So I told you earlier, the corporate entertainment part of being a Partner, I have always found tedious. But now I have become a Partner I realize that it is a necessary evil. The tricky thing is it's one of those sentiments that at least to some extent, Lauren and I share. Albeit, she hates it with more passion than me. I don't know the full story, but it has something to do with the fact that growing up, she saw more than her fair share of it, the social game, that is. I get her point. It can be a breeding ground for unauthentic conversation. As I say, I get it. I say tricky because, it was obvious this was one of those events where you needed ideally to bring your partner.

It was some golf tournament in Pebble Beach where seemingly it paired professional players with celebrities (and vertically and horizontally that was a broad term) to play in a Championship. The firm had one of those corporate marquee tents next to the last hole and was going to be serving food and drink, etc, to VIP clients, and we would host them. You get the idea. So, you will appreciate that I was completely flummoxed when Lauren accepted without anything resembling a fight. I mean a corporate client event and golf, two things that she hated. Yet, curiously, when

Sandy Nicolson

I asked her, she said, "Absolutely, I am in."

She did give me one condition, though. We had to go on her motorbike. I took that as her control thing and, of course, making a statement that she was no golfer when we arrived, I supposed. Golfers are not bikers. In fact, they hate them according to Lauren. As much as I was terrified riding on the back of that thing, and would have to work out how to pack the saddlebags smartly with our clothes. I acquiesced. Really, it was the path of least resistance.

Her Harley Davidson Heritage was her pride and joy. She was a great rider, don't get me wrong, but as you can probably tell by now, I am a control freak. Riding around San Francisco was one thing, going for, say, Sunday brunch, but driving all the way to Pebble Beach was a different proposition altogether and, most importantly, involved highways (and so going fast). Maybe a 2-hour journey, if we were lucky.

Don't get me wrong, though, over that tiramisu in a little Italian, we like off Columbus Avenue. I gave her a double take through the candle between us when I raised the invite with her. There was something too easy about it. It was almost like she expected the invite, which sounds like a funny thing to say. Maybe that is what keeps relationships going, I told myself at the time. Surprises, I supposed, but nevertheless, the fact that she made no complaint about corporate excess, greed and how unthoughtful of me to raise the idea was truly odd. There was simply no speech. There was none of her usual bluster that I knew was really a smoke screen about her nerves in having to socialize with corporate types, with whom she felt she had nothing in common.

After that dinner, I rolled our conversation over in my head and her quick acceptance as I tried to sleep. Was there something about Lauren that I hadn't noticed? I let it go and prepared myself for hanging on to the back of her for a two-hour ride to Pebble Beach of course.

When we packed the bike, she took one saddle bag, and I took the other. She insisted on no cross mingling. You know, that didn't strike me as odd, as she was always like that about everything. If I ever tried to share food with her at a restaurant or a glass of wine for a taste, no matter how hard I pushed, there would be a negative response. I would rather have my own, she would respond.

So, with the event, we had an overnight stay at the Lodge. We arrived the morning of the event.

At check-in, they gave us the program, which really meant nothing to both of us. The main page read as follows;

Sandy Nicolson

2010 Monterey Professional Amateur Invitational ("MPAI")

The organizing committee of the MPAI is delighted to announce this year's Amateur participants;

Denzel Iowa - Quarterback and hall of famer

Morgan Johnson - Actor

Robert Menendez - Journalist and presenter

Cynthia Sorensen - Actress

Martin Watson Wyatt III - Basketball player

Tina Marigold - Comedian

Bob Margot - Footballer

Joey Tuner - Soccer player

Hal Norton - Singer

Fred Jacobsen - businessman

The Party - rapper

Rod Martinez - baseball player

Gordon McPherson - actor

Barry Trotsy - Singer

Bonsai

James Hilton - writer

Manny Takeshi - businessmen and philanthropist

Lauren took a sip of her champagne, which they had given her at the hotel reception and curiously said, "You're the corporate one. Have you ever heard of this businessman?" and she passed me the summary bio to read;

Manny Takeshi

Manny Takeshi is one of the world's most successful entrepreneurs. After founding his agricultural equipment transport business here in the Salinas Valley (including transporting mowers used on this very course!) Manny went on to expand that business into one of Japan's most iconic conglomerates. With 100,000 employees in 53 countries, Takeshi Enterprises is the largest transportation business in the world. As their catchphrase goes, "You want it, we got it." Manny is also known as an incredibly generous philanthropist, and the Manny Foundation has donated approximately $250m to good causes around the world. Manny is currently a 14 handicapper and is paired this week with Sven Ulrich, from Sweden and currently the European Tour Leader.

"No, I haven't, maybe vaguely. I know the tech folks," I replied, trying to get my business pride back.

I smiled nervously and said, "Are you okay, honey? You are acting sort of weird."

"Why?" she said defensively.

"Well, that is the first time you have ever shown any interest in anything corporate?"

She smiled mischievously; "I am just trying to get into the part, my Lil. You know someone might ask me a question about him, and I don't want to get embarrassed".

"Okay, but it's really the real players you're supposed to know, and well, neither of us knows shit about that, and it's too late to cram for that exam. Let's just make like a couple of dumb broads!"

And we both laughed snarkily as we went to our room.

When we got to the room, it had taken her ten seconds to change into her trousers and golf polo shirt with my firm's corporate logo, which apparently she had to wear, and of course, she did so reluctantly. Anyway, once she dressed, she said she had to go and take a walk and look around and would be back.

As usual, it took me much longer to get ready. In my robe, I stood on the balcony, which overlooked the course. I took in the stands around the 18th green to the right of our room. I had never

Bonsai

been to a golf tournament. All at once, it made me think of the theater as I looked at the stands, and at the same time, a vision of my Dad came to me. I don't know why, other than this is probably the closest I had been to Salinas in many years, and it reminded me of following him around a golf course near here as a child, to his frustration picking up his ball prematurely.

Anyway, after that rare moment of sentimentality, I returned to the bathroom to finish getting ready, and something happened that changed my life and my relationship with Lauren forever. I went to get my toiletry bag from my saddle bag. I opened it. A leather bag with buckles on its side. There is no, at least, on Lauren's bike, a bag lock. Each one sits on either side of the Harley, and it's like a detachable suitcase. Small, but good enough for a weekend break or a corporate break if you like this. Anyway, I opened Lauren's by mistake. I absently stuffed my hand in, and it took me a minute to realize it was Lauren's. As I shuffled my hand, suddenly, I touched something cold and metallic. No! It can't be, I said to myself. I pulled it out and held it in the palms of my hands.

It was a Glock handgun. I just sat there hunkered down in my robe, staring at it. What the hell was my girlfriend, an interior designer, doing traveling to a corporate event with me with a handgun? Scratch, why on earth did she own a handgun? My whole world suddenly imploded. Like I was suddenly in some kind of quicksand sinking fast? I began to sweat a cold sweat that covered my forehead and ran down my back. I felt hives rising. What was her lie? She had been lying to me the whole time? I thought she loved me. All the time, all I could do was stare at this instrument of death in my hands, which were shaking uncontrollably. I cautiously put the gun on the floor and looked at the door furtively before diving deeper into her bag. I pulled everything out and threw every bit of its contents theatrically across the floor. A shirt, a pair of jeans, a pair of Chelsea boots, a bra, a tee shirt, a hair brush, and an iPhone charger now lay across the floor of the hotel room. It looked like a 14-year-old's bedroom. And there, at the bottom of the bag, was a small black wallet. A wallet I had never seen or noticed; I raised it out of the bag and, in slow motion, in retrospect, I opened it. Inside, there was a picture of her, looking uncharacteristically stern, and the wording like a driver's license was all around it, but instead of deciphering the numbers and words, most importantly, my eyes were drawn to the following;

    Lt Lauren Roberts

    San Francisco Police Department

    Special Operations

I immediately threw it to the floor and dragged my hands through my hair. I felt so dirty and used. How could she say she loved me and not tell me? I am a lawyer, after all. She lied to me. I

Bonsai

loved her. This jumble of thoughts rattled through my head until a crack outside brought me back to the room and the present. I quickly put the gun, with my hands still shaking, back into the bag and stuffed it in with the clothes as fast as I could. Then I heard a beep, just in time, and the door opened, and it was Lauren. She was now a completely different person to me. The interior designer Lauren had vanished, and in her place was this alien shadow, a dark shadow, this policewoman with whom I had slept so many times and told her I loved her. This was someone I bore my soul to. She was now a complete stranger to me. A terrifying stranger at that.

"Wow," she said.

"Wow?" I said, desperately trying to control my shaking.

"Yes, wow, you really haven't made much progress, have you?"

"Progress?"

"Are you okay? I mean, you've made no progress in getting ready, since I left. Take all the time you want. It's your party."

"Oh, yeah, of course," I said, steadying myself and adding by way of explanation, "Yes, I am just a little nervous about today. You know about meeting people that I don't know".

Before I knew it, my lack of progress prompted the most unwelcome invitation, and the stranger was in front of me, hugging me and trying to kiss me.

"No, not now, I said," and pushed her off and went straight to the bathroom in a whirl, where I made sure to lock the door. When I was inside, I sat on the floor and wept as quietly as I could.

Chapter 19
It Was Takeshi's Wish That You Accept This

The morning of the match, I called Monty before leaving the gas station to steady my nerves and share notes on plans for meeting after the match.

"Today is your big day, my friend. Did my "caddy man" train you as well as I said he would?"

"He did Monty, and I am eternally grateful for the introduction. This whole experience has been so out of the box that it ironically gave me something real to focus on. You know the yardages, the weather, the club choice, the pep talks you should give to your player, the reminder on etiquette, watching the crowd and overall, he said to enjoy it".

"Enjoy it, of course you should," Monty agreed.

"I haven't seen her yet, Captain, you know Ly, but I think she may be here. I asked Takeshi if she was here, and all he said abstractly was, "Not yet." I don't want to clutch at straws, but, you know, I think that might be a good sign."

"I agree with you, my friend. Now I have been thinking. And don't get nervous about this, but I want to drive you to Takeshi's this morning for the pickup. I know that from his house, you will be taking him from his house in a golf cart, and no limo is required. I was thinking last night, well, you will need a good friend to steady your nerves. I am not saying you have butterflies, but I think it would be a good thing for me to drive you there to his place. So you can gather your thoughts".

I thought for a moment; "I don't object," I said.

"I am glad you said that because I am parked outside your garage in the good old Camry."

On the drive to Takeshi's house, I told my friend blow-by-blow what had happened the day before, which he listened to intently without speaking. The walk down memory lane at the Pacific Grove turn-off, the sight of the Porsche, the airplane strip, the helicopter and the conversation on Pfeiffer Beach.

When we got there, I waved our participants' badge at the Pebble Beach gate security guard, who looked at the car and both of us again. Not surprisingly, he took his time to ensure the badge's authenticity. Before us and behind us were all sorts of exotic cars; Ferraris, Rolls Royces etc, so I get it: we were in a 1993 Toyota Camry. I couldn't say this, but thanks to me, this particular Camry ran like a dream. Eventually, they let us through, and when it was clear we were pulling close to Takeshi's house, all Monty said was simply, "I know this may seem strange, but just try and have fun today, my friend. If nothing else, this is a once-in-a-lifetime experience that most people would die for".

I reached over my hand and shook his.

"Also," he added," I will be watching. So, you will be safe."

I smiled back nervously.

As I walked up the drive to Takeshi's house, I looked up at it, and the house seemed to radiate a different light. Like it had been woken from a great sleep. I realized at the top of the steps where the housekeeper used to stand was the Adviser. He was standing there in his usual uniform (black suit and white shirt and aviators) but as I got closer, I realized he was looking much more stern than the last interactions I had with him.

"Mister Bonsai:" he greeted me.

"Good morning:" I ventured.

I was now a step below him, looking up. He hadn't moved a muscle this whole time.

I could see he was holding another of his white envelopes in his hands.

"I am afraid it is not such a good morning, Mister Bonsai."

My head raced. What was that Takeshi reference when I asked about Ly; "not yet?" Did this mean that something bad happened to Ly, and it was just a matter of time before he told me. I froze and listened intently to the Advisers' next words.

"Unfortunately, last night, Mister Takeshi left this world. He passed away peacefully. You see, he was suffering from a terrible disease. I know this will be heavy news for you, as it is, of course, for me".

I tried to digest what all this meant and if it closed the door on finding out what had happened to Ly and where she was, never mind seeing her again. You will appreciate my heart sank for different reasons.

I realized he was offering me the white envelope, again with the Takeshi crest emblazoned on the front, and as I took it in my hands, I realized it was the same expensive paper, of course.

The Adviser continued to speak as I took hold of it.

"Mister Takeshi had some final wishes. He knew that he had been an inconvenience to you already in more ways than one. He thought very highly of you".

I felt like swearing at him then, but I let him go on.

"He has two final wishes, that he would like you to posthumously accept. He hoped you would. The first is documented in the envelope which you should open with your friend who, as I

Bonsai

can see through the hedge row, is still there in that Toyota of his'".

I turned, and through the hedgerow, sure enough, the Camry was still visible through the shrubbery at the end of the front yard.

"Please go now and consider it with your friend. Lastly, and importantly, if you do accept his offer, he very much requests you to return here tomorrow morning after sunrise for his last and final act, if you will. Anyway, I won't keep you because you must catch your friend in case he leaves".

And with that, with his usual footwork catwalk precision, he had turned back inside the house, and the front door closed behind him with a click.

My brain had too many thoughts to process, and so I found myself nodding in acceptance and running back to the Camry.

"You didn't leave," I said to my surprised friend as I opened the door, slightly out of breath.

"I hope you don't think bad of me, but I wanted to make sure you were okay."

"Well, I am glad you didn't. Takeshi is dead. Died last night apparently".

The Captain looked at me with an incredulous look on his face. Wow, it said.

"And as you will see, I have another of these treasure hunt things," I said, referring to the envelope in front of me. The Captain gave me a look that said, "Go on, open it."

So, I did, and inside, this is what it said, which I read aloud to my friend;

"My dear Bonsai,

You now know I will not be able to make my tee time today, or ever for that matter.

Like this note, I am afraid life is one big mystery. Frequently, that means people have to do things or things happen they do not understand. In my experience, one thing is true: like you said, the sun and moon will be constant. If I may add, good and evil, too are constants. I cannot apologize completely for everything I have done, nor can you. Sometimes, destiny plays its part. In that regard, I believe we did not have a choice.

I have a final ask of you. I have arranged for you to take my place at the match today. It will be billed as a remarkable thing by the media, don't let that phase you. "The celebrity has his caddy take his place," the headlines will read. All the right people are prepared to accept that. Trust me. If he is willing, I humbly suggest you ask your good friend to caddy for you. Then, on completion of your round, which I hope you enjoy, tomorrow morning, I would like

Bonsai

you to go to the Rose Garden at my house after sunrise, the reason will be revealed to you there and then. My apologies for being so cryptic, but it is necessary, and I believe you will find the outcome of all of this most satisfying to you.

Believe me, there quite simply could be no other way.

And with that, I must go now. I will not be around to know the outcome of these requests, but I do hope the right conclusion is achieved for the sake of balance in the universe.

Hit them straight.

Takeshi-san"

I closed the envelope and tried to take it all in.

It was dumbfounded.

My friend, steady as ever, just looked at me from the steering wheel of the Camry with a smile and said, "Have you ever played Pebble before?"

The levity made me smile, "Do you think your leg will hold up?" I returned, and we drove to the Lodge.

Chapter 20

Lauren Discovers The Wild Goose Chase, And Lily Finds What She Lost

I left Lily to get ready in the hotel room. Fortunately, she always took forever to get changed. When I got to the carpark, sure enough, the Ford Transit van with the National Network Sign emblazoned on its side was next to "The Big Al" tour bus, right where I was told to find it. I knocked on the rear door three times. In short order, the doors opened, and I was soon inside with Blake and one of his detectives, whom I knew vaguely from another assignment. We exchanged our hellos.

The inside of the van wasn't much different. In fact, it was probably the same as a regular television network van at these types of events. There were wall-to-wall monitors in front of them, presently projecting images from different greens, fairways and tee boxes from around the course.

"You think you're a Sports Television Producer, don't you?" I said.

"You got me, another missed career, Lauren."

"Anyway, I don't have much time. I need to get back to my girlfriend, who is getting ready. I think I told you my cover for this was perfect as my girlfriend's law firm has a corporate event here to which I was invited".

"You at a corporate event? That I have to see," replied Blake with a smile.

"Anyway," Blake continued, "Takeshi should be here anytime soon. His tee-off is at 10 am. He is playing with a Swedish player in the top 20 in the World, but I suspect you couldn't care less about that. So the plan is to play it really cool. Track him around to make sure there is no funny stuff. Then, when the round is done, you escort him off on the pretext of an interview and we will take care of the rest. However, I do have one major reservation."

"What is that?"

Blake looked at me sternly, like my High School principal when I lied about taking off school.

"You know fine well Lauren."

I stayed quiet.

"The caddy, the gas station workers' daughter, Lily, is your girlfriend, isn't she?"

I stayed perfectly still. Not a muscle in my body was moving, and I struggled to concentrate. All I could think of was her waiting for me in the bedroom and wondering where I had gone.

Sandy Nicolson

We endured a moment of excruciating silence before Blake broke it.

"I'll be candid with you. It's actually because of that that I am letting you continue with this assignment. We found nothing about her father except that he was once Takeshi's driver in the 1970's. So, you are a smart person. Maybe your presence might actually bring something on that to the front".

"So, you are using me, Captain?"

"Don't be cute with me, and thank your lucky stars, as this could be a lot worse, withholding that sort of information from me. Anyway, we will talk about it later. Meantime, Justin here will check your ear plug is working for the course, and then you better get back to your corporate introductions before you head out on the course. 10 am, I told you, is the tee-off time for Takeshi".

I gave Blake a look that said, I understand and thank you.

When I got back to the room, Lily was acting strange. She didn't want to kiss me and then locked herself in the bathroom. As we walked to the corporate tent, I was hoping this was going to be a simple dodge for me from the event at the last minute, but her frosty mood was going to make this difficult, so just before we reached the tent, I mistakenly confronted her.

"What is wrong? What's wrong with you? Is it nerves?"

Then she slapped me. A full-blown slap that made my face wring.

"What the f !"

Then she was screaming.

"You lied to me. ALL THIS TIME! You're not an interior designer. I thought you designed coffee shops. I was so stupid. I feel so stupid. You're a COP".

I quickly grabbed her and put my hand over her mouth and held one of her hands firmly behind her back and hissed in her ear.

"This is not the time for this, Lily, it really isn't. If it is not obvious, I am actually working now. I couldn't tell you before. I will tell you. But just not now".

I could feel her warm tears run across my hand that was covering her mouth. I cursed myself for being so sloppy. She must have looked in my bag. I was sore about her being upset but I needed to get out of this and back on with the job. The Rolex clock behind her said the time. It was 9.30 am and only 30 minutes until the tee-off.

"When I take my hand away, are you going to be cool?"

She nodded reluctantly.

"I was going to "slope" off from the event to do my job, but

I will be more honest with you. I am going now, and I need you to be okay. I will explain everything. I promise afterward. Can you nod to say you're okay? Can you do that for me?"

She nodded reluctantly and wiped her tears with her hand, smudging her makeup, which looked out of place anyway.

Then she looked at me in a way she had never done before. I can only describe it as a poker face and said coldly, "It is fine. Really, it is fine. I am used to it. Everyone I have tried to love has lied to me".

With that, she turned and headed towards the corporate tents.

I steadied myself and went the other way toward the first tee. I hustled my way to the front of the tee box and cooly checked in on my audio with Blake and Justin to check everything was in order.

As I waited there, I tried to steady my emotions. If I was going to save our relationship, it was going to be complicated, though. Not only would I have to explain my real profession and why I lied, but the whole dynamic of our relationship was based on something more deeply false than that. I had allowed her to think I was the vulnerable one and she was the dominant, strong one, when really, well, not really, that was actually completely untrue. Did that taint everything we had ever done? Our conversations, her thoughts for me, her picture of who she thought I was? But then, she wanted a cliche. She could have looked harder, couldn't she? Was she the one who was self-obsessed in her own career and life? She should have spotted it! Then there was the fact that it would soon be obvious that I was tracking her father and knew something about her mother that I never shared with her as soon as I found out. I was screwed when I thought of it that way.

The tee box announcer broke me from my internal marriage counseling conversation. Crap, I was working, I needed to concentrate. As I did so, as I tuned in to what I expected to be a perfunctory announcement, to my horror I realized it was anything but.

"Ladies and Gentleman, for the fifth tee-off of the day we have a special announcement. There has been a change to this grouping. An important change.

Bizarrely, the announcer paused. This was completely unlike the other non-descript tee-off announcements. The pause was very theatrical.

The crowd hushed.

I spoke into my microphone, "Something is going on here. Something strange. Hold on. Over".

After what seemed an age, the announcer continued.

"It is with deepest sadness to inform you that the celebrity in this group, the wonderful Manny Takeshi-San passed away in the early hours of this morning".

The crowd cried out in dismay (like they even knew who he was).

"It was Mister Takeshi-San's dying wish that his caddy, a keen golfer and lifelong friend, play in his stead. After careful consideration, the Championship Committee has decided that in these exceptional circumstances, to permit a dying man's wish, a lover and great benefactor to golf, especially in Japan, yes out of respect to him and the ethos of our sport, we have granted his request. So, with all the respect to Manny Takeshi, rest in peace and with tremendous respect to his dear friend for taking his place at such short notice and under such difficult circumstances. May I welcome you to the tee, and please give a warm welcome to the one known affectionately as Bonsai!"

At this point, the crowd went completely wild!!! The round of applause took nearly ten minutes to die down. Lily's father stood not more than 5 meters away from me on the first tee, swishing his driver theatrically. At one point, he actually looked at me. Beside him was an old black guy who seemed to be his friend. The whole thing was beyond surreal.

I felt like I was going to be sick.

Bonsai

I could hear Blake swear in my ear.

Meantime, Lily was in the marquee with all of her corporate clients. She was trying desperately to compartmentalize her life, and she had created a new box in her mind's storage facility titled; "Lauren." She visualized a big wooden box in a storage facility. Maybe the Met storage facility or some sort of old museum like that and the caretaker wheeling the coffin-sized wooden box down through the warehouse. Wooden boxes were stacked high as the ceilings on either side in her mind's eye.

When the caretaker got to the appropriate spot. He slid the box off his trolley. Once it was in a place like the piece of a Jenga puzzle, you could now clearly see the stamp; "Lauren," and on the box next to it, of course, was one labeled; "Mom."

Lily had shaken herself from doing her internal filing and concentrated on socializing. Something she needed full concentration on, as you know now, it was neither something she was good at nor comfortable with. So she took a sip of her Mimosa they had handed to her and looked at the room. There were maybe 40 or 50 people in the marquee 50:50 clients to Partners. All around the tent were television screens, of course, and live footage from different holes. The idea was they would have breakfast in the tent and then head out onto the course and sit in various VIP sections in designated spots in the stands.

Lily scanned the room and randomly picked a large bald man in his late 60s who had just got a plate of food and so was unchaperoned presently.

"Hi:" she introduced herself.

She looked at his name lanyard; "Duke Roberts - CEO - Roberts Investments LLC."

They exchanged small talk about golf and this and that. There was something about his face that was somewhat familiar, Lily had thought, but she let it pass at first.

"So, you live in San Francisco," he was saying, "I have a daughter that lives there…..but you know we don't talk. She's a cop. A complete and utter waste of her life. She had the brains to be a lawyer like you but, you know, wasted it. Blames me for so many things. Woman. No offense". He commentated and downed his mimosa in one gulp and then wiped his nose.

Just as he was asking Lily what school she went to. Suddenly, chaos broke out in the tent, and someone shouted turn it up, then louder, turn up the televisions !!!

Lily tried to tune in to what was going on around her. The volume of the television in the marquee was deafening. Lily felt like a cat that had been spooked.

Bonsai

She tuned in to what the television commentator was telling the room;

"Have we ever seen anything like this in professional sport? This is truly remarkable. A man dies and gives his place to his dear friend. A magnate of industry, one of the richest men in the world, and we are still researching, but this friend of his, get this, this is incredible, he owns a gas station near here, I believe, Salinas? This has the makings of a fairytale, Nick, it really does.

Doesn't it just, and what incredible things does it say about our sport?"

Lily had dropped the glass of Mimosa she was holding, her lower lip hat hit the carpet, too, and she was looking at the screens all around the room. Completely mesmerized, stunned, freaked, there isn't a strong enough word to describe it, as she realized she, along with all of her Partners and the largest tech company bosses, and the crowd at Pebble Beach, and the World were all looking, at well, at Bonsai !!! And the most crazy thing for Lily was he had a strut in his gait and, most of all, remarkably, he was smiling! Something that Lily found herself doing, too. She couldn't help it if she tried.

Sandy Nicolson

Chapter 21

Never mind the leaders; we are following a different story, folks

Television Network Feed - Commentary Excerpts From The Match

Commentary 10.05 am

UNBELIEVABLE. There has just been the most remarkable announcement, we are all just picking ourselves off the floor here, and it's not because of a golf shot. Manny Takeshi, a Japanese businessman, one of the richest men in the world, passed away last night. Our deepest condolences are with him and his family. Remarkably, his caddy will be playing in his place. This is unprecedented.

Commentary 10.07

Now his caddy is handing him his driver!

Commentary 10.09

Let's imagine the pressure on this man. Playing with one of the hottest golfers on the tour at the moment. Never mind that his friend has just died, he has been given a place in the tournament, and he is driving down the first at Pebble, with millions watching. Can you even begin to imagine as he stands over his drive, what on earth

Bonsai

must be going through his head?

Commentary 10.11

And what a roar the crowd has given this unknown man. There is a hush. We look on anxiously. We have all been there. Don't duff it. We are all thinking but not saying! There, I said it. Whoosh. And it is flush down the middle. He picks up his tee like a seasoned professional. This is extraordinary!

Commentary 10.45

We are getting reports that not only was this man Takeshi's friend, it seems, now hold on folks, this is beyond any superlative, he is a gas station worker from nearby Salinas who plays local clubs. That's right, not Pebble Beach. This must be his first round and he probably only dreamed of playing here until today and get this, so far, he is playing it like a computer game.

Commentary 11.15

We now have another remarkable report coming in. This Bonsai chaps' caddy today is a retired Marine Captain. One of the first African American men to attain the rank. He served 5 tours before retiring to Monterey Country to teach. And these guys are golfing buddies. You seriously could not make this up. If this doesn't bring a tear to your eye, I really don't know what would.

Sandy Nicolson

Commentary 12.07

As we head towards the turn, we are seeing something remarkable here. We have completely and unashamedly, with all due respect, lost our usual focus on the leaders to follow a once-in-a-lifetime story being played out in front of us. Not that it really matters in the scheme of things, but he really is playing a round that he can be proud of. He is a 20 handicapper, for goodness sake, and his best buddy just died. But you know, despite all that, respectfully, they are enjoying it. You can tell.

Commentary 1.47

Kudos to the Championship committee for allowing this to happen. And respect to this Swedish professional, Bonsai is paired with. He is showing a lot of class handling the obvious attention this group is getting here. If anything, I think the Swede is trying to control his nerves.

Commentary 2.05

You know, I think there is something touching that Bonsai's caddy suit has "Takeshi" on the back. I am sure he is up there watching this play out, and he should be proud of himself for making it happen for his friend and all of you at home. It reminds us all of what golf should be about. That is right, the game, the course and above all, enduring friendship.

Commentary 2.30

What an emotional rollercoaster this has been. We are not sure who this is, but there is a girl who has walked onto the 17th tee box. Security looked to be coming across, but Bonsai is gesturing to say it's okay. He has just given her a hug. Golly, it's a long one. Hug, that is. I think we all want to give him that hug. Maybe it's his daughter?

Commentary 2.34

WOW, what a shot! The Swede gives Bonsai a deserved high five, without doubt, his best shot of the day. One even Nicklaus would be proud of!

Commentary 2.50

Forget Tiger at the Masters. I have never seen such a rousing reception on 18 at Pebble in my life. Both of these gentlemen are really enjoying their moment as they walked down the 18th. Quite right. There are waves to the crowds. We all have so much respect for these gentlemen right now. I, for one, am emotionally spent here.

Commentary 2.52

The Swede holes his putt to finish the round in with a respectable 68 and combined score of 1 under par, which, all things considered, is truly exceptional. Bonsai and his friend high-five each other. And there is the same lady we saw on the 17th tee box. She is now on the 18th green and hugging Bonsai again. Yes, we can confirm that is his daughter. This is very touching. She has just handed something to him. It looks like a card. It can't be, but I can't be sure, but it looks like a business card.

Commentary 2.54

Well, that was something, a day we simply won't forget. Thank you, Bonsai and friend, you have uplifted us all and thank you, Takeshi-san, rest in peace now.

Chapter 22

Meet me in the Rose Garden

Believe it or not, after the day of all days, I woke up in my own bed above my gas station. I will admit it, though, I have no idea how I got to bed. I lay there and took in all facets of the day. Monty, being kind enough to take out the early nerves by driving me to Takeshi's, receiving the news from the Adviser, opening the envelope with Monty, asking him to caddy and his acceptance, meeting all the players, the first tee, the roar from the crowd, the anxiousness over the first drive, my breathing, hanging in there with a few pars and a few birdies, then the moment it happened. Did it really happen? It feels like a dream. The vision of Lily coming out of the crowd on the 17th tee and hugging me will last forever in my memory. Then my shot on 17th to five feet. It induced a high five from one of the greatest golfers. And then walking up 18 with my best friend to endless cheers. Lastly, well, maybe the perfect finish, Lily telling me;

"Enjoy it, Dad, I am proud of you. Call me when you can". And in perfect Lily style, giving me her business card. It was truly the perfect day.

I picked up the card beside my bed and held it above my head and read it again and again.

Sandy Nicolson

As the sun poked through my dirty curtains, I realized, in all the excitement, I had forgotten the Adviser's other note and Takeshi's final wish, the Rose Garden request.

I quickly changed. It was still really early. When I opened the door of the store, though, I had never seen anything like it. There was a forest of paparazzi and television network vans out front. I fought through the scrum as politely as I could as they took my picture. They were shouting at me, things like.

"Can we speak for a moment, please?"

"How did it feel yesterday?"

"How much does Captain Montgomerie mean to you?"

"How much did you love Takeshi?"

"When did you last see your daughter?"

I finally got to my old Ford pickup and brought it to life, and headed for the 101, narrowly avoiding a photographer as I barrelled out to Takeshi's house. I hadn't driven there in the old Ford in such haste since Lily was about to be born.

Going the other way on the highway, North toward San Francisco, was truck after truck with all the stands, portaloos and equipment from the event on their backs. As I looked at them, it felt surreal to have been part of it all. Like they had already dismantled

Bonsai

part of my life but I had a memory that would last forever.

I was conscious there was a convoy of media vans behind me, but I knew that when I got to Pebble Beach and waived my badge, they likely wouldn't be able to follow me. Which thankfully proved to be true.

Once I got into the park, I felt myself able to breathe again. I then began to realize I had no idea what this cryptic meet in the rose garden actually meant. I suddenly got a little self-conscious about my clothes. I realized I was still wearing my golf clothes from the day before. Oh well, if I was going to be killed and I was racing toward my death, maybe, there were no more appropriate clothes to be buried in.

I pulled the truck in at almost the same spot the Camry was at yesterday and walked toward the gate. I afforded myself an indulgent look at the now empty golf course and smiled ruefully remembering the shots I played on that hole.

When I looked up the drive, the Adviser was waiting for me at the entrance. Oddly, too, the Emerald Green Porsche 911T was in the drive. I glanced at it as I walked toward the Adviser.

"Congratulations, Bonsai. What a day yesterday. I know Mister Takeshi-San would be most pleased. His wish came true".

I smiled. "Is he still here, so to speak, I asked?"

"No, he has been returned to Japan," he said curtly and moved on quickly. He looked at me up and down with a slight look of concern. He said quickly, "Now let me show you upstairs so you can take a shower, and there is a change of clothes for you." Before I could disagree with him, I was following him upstairs, and he showed me into this huge bedroom with gallery windows that looked straight out to the Pacific and the eagerly rising sun.

"I took the liberty of choosing some clothes for you, and the shower is running. Once you are finished, please find your way to the rose garden, where tea is being served:"

A warm shower would be nice, I thought. I nodded, and the Adviser left me alone.

I showered. It was a wonderful, warm, soapy shower. The shower had jets that shot out water from all angles. I have never had a shower like that, and I have never felt as clean as I did afterward. I didn't feel tired anymore. Instead, I felt invigorated. In fact, I don't think I have ever felt so alive.

I used some of the cologne that had been left out on a marble countertop and even put on a little talcum powder.

I dressed in the change of clothes the Adviser had selected for me and almost on some sort of autopilot. I could instantly feel the quality of the expensive fabrics on my clean skin. He even left a

Bonsai

pair of sunglasses for me. A pair of aviators.

As I descended the imperial staircase en route to the rose garden, I caught sight of myself briefly in the large mirror that framed the wall. Absent-mindedly, I noticed I was wearing a white blazer, black pants and a pair of Raybans but thought nothing of it.

When I got to the French doors that led to the garden, the Adviser was waiting. He said;

"Can I get you some tea?"

"That would be great," I said.

"You know where to find it, the Rose Garden?"

I nodded and headed into the garden. To get there, you had to walk through a trellis of white roses that were all in bloom. I arrived, and it was just me. A hummingbird flew past my nose. I was no longer living in reality, so I think I had stopped questioning these passages of events. I had certainly stopped feeling anxious a long time ago. I took a seat on a bench that was next to a gentle water feature, and as I sat there, I noticed a row of Bonsai trees around the foot of the rose bushes. I don't know how long I had been sitting there, when I heard footsteps, which I figured must be the Adviser coming with the tea.

As the footsteps grew closer, I realized they were too light to be his.

Sandy Nicolson

I looked up, and in a white dress, framed by the white roses, looking at me with the Pfeiffer Falls welcome look on was her. It was Ly. I removed the sunglasses. We looked at each other, and we were one again. We held each other's gaze until, finally, she said,

"Shall we invite our daughter for brunch?"

"A picnic at Lovers Point?" I suggested.

The End

Bonsai

Postscript

Back in the spring, San Francisco had typically mercurial weather. One day, it was wet. One day, it was foggy. One day, it was warm. One day, it was cold.

The day after she gave the ticket to him, it was one of those freezing cold days. He got kicked off the Muni at midnight and went from doorway to doorway on Market Street, frequently getting moved on by the police. He was naturally just trying to find some heat. He had managed to accumulate $4 and 25c in quarters from small finds under the cable track, the gutter and the benches next to the Harbor building. So, as the sun rose, he headed to the gas station on Third, and he had a hankering for a carton of milk. He passed a bank on the corner on his way, and it triggered a memory of another life before the financial crisis. He remembered his wife, his children, his desk, his job, his purpose, a different world. When he got to the gas station, its neon sign invited a 24-hour party, but otherwise, the forecourt was dead. Not another person or car in sight. He opened the door of the store, and the attendant looked at him and he could tell she was deciding what to do. Bored? She obviously was, and this was the first "customer" for hours, but he did look very rough though.

He hadn't shaved in, well, he had forgotten for how long. His hair looked like an abandoned bird's nest, and his old Burberry raincoat was so used it was like someone had sailed across the Atlantic in it. His goodwill store pants had maybe been used for golf 60 years ago, and his right big toe was escaping through the roof of his shoe. You get the picture. He looked like a pirate.

Yup, she was definitely thinking, do I throw him out already or see what he has to say to amuse me? That is what she was most likely weighing up, he thought. In some ways, though, his entrance was a welcome break from her college homework.

"Don't worry! I have money," he said.

He shuffled to the front desk and pulled his milk quarters from every pocket he had, including his shirt breast pocket and rained them onto the counter individually. As he yanked at his left raincoat pocket, trying to find the last one, he felt an envelope in his hand. He pulled it out. It was from the lady on the Muni. "Good Luck!" she had said dryly as she left it in his hand. He remembered her and what was inside it.

He pulled out Bonsai's lottery ticket and presented it proudly to the gas station worker. The pile of quarters sat gleaming below his outstretched hand like a pile of silver bursting with promise…….

Cut to black

About The Author

This is the first novel by Alexander "Sandy" Nicolson. The inspiration to write Bonsai came following a bone marrow transplant as part of a treatment plan for incurable (at least today) blood cancer. After a long career in consulting globally, Sandy realized it was maybe now or never to fulfill his dream of writing a novel.

Sandy is originally from Scotland and lives in California with his Australian wife, son born in England, and their mischievous American beagle, Princess Leia.

Printed in Great Britain
by Amazon

57cac3ae-7772-4ae1-8f83-116b5d53621fR02